PRAISE FOR CURTIS WHITE

"Witheringly smart, grotesquely funny, grimly comprehensive, and so moving as to be wrenching."—David Foster Wallace

"Curtis White writes out of an admirable intellectual sophistication combined with viscerality, pain, and humor."—John Barth

"Like many other satirists . . . White is a moralist. . . . He also has the candor and—more important—the writerly grace never to let his characters' high-octane, obsessive monologues slide into leaden didacticism."—Chris Lehmann, *Washington Post*

"Current American fiction has not been lacking in its awareness of television's grim effect on families, but nowhere has this theme been exploited quite so well as in Curtis White's *Memories of My Father Watching TV*."—William Ferguson, *New York Times*

OTHER BOOKS BY CURTIS WHITE

Anarcho-Hindu
Heretical Songs
The Idea of Home
Memories of My Father Watching TV
Metaphysics in the Midwest
The Middle Mind: Why Americans Don't Think for Themselves
Monstrous Possibility: An Invitation to Literary Politics
Requiem

AMERICA'S
MAGIC MOUNTAIN
A NOVEL

CURTIS WHITE

DALKEY ARCHIVE PRESS

NORMAL · LONDON

Library of Congress Cataloging-in-Publication Data

White, Curtis, 1951-
    America's magic mountain / by Curtis White.— 1st Dalkey Archive ed.
    p. cm.
    ISBN 1-56478-369-3 (alk. paper)
    1. Drinking of alcoholic beverages—Fiction. 2. Alcoholics—Rehabilitation—Fiction. 3. Rehabilitation centers—Fiction. 4. Health resorts—Fiction. 5. Alcoholics—Fiction. 6. Young men—Fiction. I. Title.

PS3573.H4575A83 2004
813'.54—dc22

                                                          2004052736

Partially funded by grants from the Lannan Foundation
and the Illinois Arts Council, a state agency.

Dalkey Archive Press is a nonprofit organization located at Milner Library
(Illinois State University) and distributed in the UK by
Turnaround Publisher Services Ltd. (London).

www.centerforbookculture.org

For ACOAs, with deep respect for your stories.

"The pure products of America go crazy."
—William Carlos Williams

1

An unassuming young man was traveling north by train from his home in Downstate, Illinois. When I say that this young man was "unassuming," I mean not merely that he assumed nothing about where he was going or what might happen to him once he got there, but that he *could* assume almost nothing, because—as our story will make clear—he *knew* little of the world outside of the absurdly narrow purview provided by textbooks in what was called Industrial Psychology. This is not, however, to say that this young man lacked intelligence. To understand his capacities one has only to imagine the possibility of a boy whose life consisted of being shoved from box to box: from the home box to the school box to the college-dorm box and now, finally, to the very edge of the factory box. In this he was not a lot different from American boys and girls of other eras past and future. That he never ventured forth from any of these boxes—until this momentous trip by train—says something only about his willingness to trust and, yes, his essential timidity.

At any rate, break forth he had now, for he planned a two-week stay at a recovery spa. The Elixir was tucked in among a squat range of mountains, or mountain-like things, more like hills, that had been formed by the slag heaps left behind by a now-vanished coal industry. Our young man, Hans Castorp, wasn't very clear about this place to which he journeyed other than that it was not far from the railroad line that ran between St. Louis and Chicago, and that he was to get off at the first stop after Dwight. Oddly, the stop didn't have a name.

The Elixir itself was located near Coal City. Its peculiar history is at the center of much of our story. Regional spas and their cures were being featured on the covers of every upscale magazine in the country. Investment analysts regularly marveled at the performance of stocks associated with the treatment of what the popular press called "boutique diseases." These diseases gave the wealthy an exhilarating sense of their own romantic participation in the suffering caused by the New Global Order's tendency to rub humanity raw. For example, one of these diseases, officially designated by the American Medical Association and classified as a kind of neuralgia, produced symptoms including a "feigned logical regression," with the prognosis that the "supranational subject will finally fail to integrate itself in the communicative order leading to a precarious solution." This "precarious solution" meant nothing other than what we used to call death. In the end, the sentimentality of death had no role in the medical science of the New Order. We're better off, the medical establishment decided, without the complicated concept of death; it just made citizens nervous and reluctant to participate in the marvels of the present.

At any rate, the response to these medical crises was, naturally, to provide more intense privileges for the rich. That much at least was as it had ever been. Thus the birth of the modern spa, places where the ultra-rich could escape their weighty responsibilities. Of course, such matters were arranged differently in Illinois. Chicagoland's wealthy and privileged were still perfectly capable of jetting off to resorts in the vestiges of New England's caterpillar-tattered forests. Nonetheless, for whatever obscure reason, a state like Illinois will have its own blue-collar (if also laughable) equivalent of whatever it imagines that the rich have. And so with money from one subterranean state agency (a special bureau in Fish and Game) and the generous contributions of the DeKalb Soybean Foundation, The Elixir was established. It promptly filled with Illinois's purest products.

Our young man, however, had to take one marvel at a time. And at just this point he was wondering about the world that sped by his train window. His trip crossed only one kind of country, the country of corn. Being a finally bright (if "boxed") young man, he wondered why a country composed entirely of corn was called a prairie. Who ate all this corn? People must eat an awful lot of cornflakes and corn bread. Certainly, much more than he ate.

Hans Castorp sat alone on the train, his tawdry and antique American Tourister suitcase—a present from his aunt—at his side. He'd thought at first that his aunt had given him a sort of family heirloom in this old luggage. He was touched by the gesture and it was part of the reason he'd been willing to make this trip. Later, though, he found the illuminating name "Jaime Flores, Wicker Park, Chicago" written with crude black marker on the inside. The thing smelled of the Salvation Army.

His aunt was, in fact, largely responsible for this trip. She was concerned about her son Ricky, who was a resident at The Elixir. Hans was astonished by the urgency of her request. He couldn't quite comprehend it. She was "concerned" for Ricky? Even though she was not willing to make the trip herself, his aunt was perhaps expressing a very late-in-developing vestigial human feeling: Care. Bless her for it, whatever the particulars of her own past (to which we'll come in due time). Still, we shouldn't be surprised if Hans found the idea a bit alien. At any rate, his aunt's concern was an acceptable excuse for doing what Hans wanted to do anyway: go on a post-graduation adventure and see the world (to the degree that a boy such as he would know how to do such a thing).

As with most other things in his life, young Hans had not imagined, let alone intended, that this trip would be serious. No. I cannot claim, nor should we imagine, that Hans was "serious." For example, he had entered Industrial Psychology not because it interested him but because his college advisor had recommended that he study IP, and Hans could not understand why he would bother to seek advice if he weren't going to take it. And nothing about his trip to this point should have provoked him to seriousness in spite of his aunt's surprising anxiety. There was a monotony of corn and soy beans on all sides. The only visible thing that was other than field was that which gave the fields some definition: withered, degraded, contemptible culverts and gullies where a few morose creatures—bug-eyed raccoons like war-orphan-poster-children—were reduced to a life of crepuscular and barnacle-like clinging. But Hans was a boy who knew nothing more about what the land ought to look like than we do. Then as now, the land was under the burden of centuries of human intent.

Soon, the oceans of corn engendered a certain forgetfulness. A certain obliviousness. A certain opaqueness. The sheer vastness of the spectacle distanced him from his ordinary reality. His future employment to begin soon with the Caterpillar Company of Peoria,

Illinois, eternal manufacturers of behemoth earth-moving devices, seemed to him now implausible. For the moment, he was breathing the same air as farmers, people who lived in a way he could barely imagine.

The train sailed this ocean of corn in which these curious farmers waded. It passed wretched little towns and wretched larger towns: Towanda, Lexington, Ballard, Chenoa, Ocoya, Pontiac and Odell. It was a world where vinyl siding, the last-gasp effort at decency, was all dented and peeling and fallen and faded. It was wholly solemn and disappointing and this was not lost on our dweller-among-college-dorms.

At last, the train came to a station, a very small station, in fact nothing more than a collapsing brick shack. The conductor came by removing seat checks from overhead, including Hans's.

"Are we here already?" asked Hans.

The conductor smiled. It was a smile both tense and relaxed. It was the habitual smile of train conductors. It expressed boredom, disdain, petty privilege, laziness, and anxiety. "Here?" he loomed, "where is *here* for you, son?"

Hans heard this question very literally. It didn't make sense to him. "Where is *here* for you?" What could such a question mean?

The conductor tried to be more helpful. "Where are you going?"

"Oh, my aunt has asked me to see my cousin Ricky."

Now the disdainful part of the smile became truly magnificent. "And where is Ricky?"

"Ricky's at The Elixir."

The conductor returned brusquely to collecting tickets, muttering bitterly in his wake, "This is it. Get off here."

But, for our boy, being told to get off here seemed dangerous. Okay, the train trip had been fine, but what was outside the train? The little station looked dead. It was a very gray world. Perhaps it was just the dirty window. He opened it and looked outside, but if anything the air was even dirtier, like looking through dusty cheesecloth. He was almost relieved not to see his cousin. But there, indeed, at last, loping through the gloom, was an older version of the boy Hans clearly remembered as his cousin.

"Hans," Ricky yelled, "get off."

But something deep was speaking to Hans. "Don't get off," a voice said. "This is the Village of the Damned."

Hans yelled back to his cousin, "This is not the place, Ricky! This is not where I'm going!"

"Yes, this is it, for God's sake. Why else am I here? Hurry! The train only pauses at this station."

"No! This can't be it!"

"Get off the train, Hans, or you'll end up in Joliet, or worse, Chicago."

Chicago. Beirut with baseball. A place of unspeakable horror for Industrial Psychology majors. Hans grabbed his luggage and hurried for the door.

When Ricky greeted him, there were no hugs or even handshakes. Ricky clicked his heels in a vaguely military gesture that seemed strange to Hans since he was aware that Ricky's gloomy condition made him 4-F. It only made sense in that Ricky had always had a fondness for guns and shooting things, especially little birds. When Hans heard stories on TV about endangered species, the grisly little corpses that had fallen to Ricky's youthful BB gun would flash before his mind.

"It's been a long time since then, eh, Cousin?" asked Ricky, winking absurdly.

That was a strange thing to say, thought Hans. Since when? What
"then" did Ricky refer to?

"Yes, it has been a long time, Ricky," he replied. Hans reached
for his cousin's shoulder to give him a hug. He wished to establish
a feeling of warmth. Ricky accepted his hug, but when their cheeks
touched Hans recoiled. There was something cold and wet about
Ricky's skin. It was as if his face were made of pastry dough.

A taxi driver was looking on as the two young men greeted each
other. He had a large badge that spelled out NGUMBE. He seemed
anxious to get Hans and Ricky to a cab. But before he could, another
black man, a Haitian, came up and began arguing with him. Hans
read his tag. LA CHENIER. The two men seemed just embarked
on a long dialogue destined to steadily grow and expand. It was obviously going to end up somewhere very messy. They had just reached
the index-finger-to-the-chest stage of discussion when a third man,
a Middle-Eastern man, stood up from a group of five who crouched
beneath blankets by the wall of the tiny, collapsing brick station. He
walked over calmly, took Hans's suitcase and then walked toward
what Hans had assumed was the first man's taxi. He hurled the suitcase in through the open passenger-side window and got behind the
steering wheel.

Ricky looked on. "We'd better go with him, old boy, if you ever
want to see your suitcase again."

While Ngumbe and the Haitian remained locked in their idiotic
debate, the cousins got in the back of the taxi.

"Don't these men each have their own cabs?"

Ricky lit a cigarette and looked at Hans with the bemusement of a veteran. "Not here, old boy. Not here."

"But what gives this homeless man, if that is what he is, the right to drive this taxi?"

"Any one of them could, if they dared. It's all in what you have the nerve for here."

"But those drunks there . . . ?"

"Easy, Cousin. We shouldn't aggravate the situation. He'll get us home safely." Ricky smiled at his cousin. It was a perplexing smile. Hans could not tell if it was reassuring or malicious. He could not tell if his cousin's smile was telling him something about where he was beginning his adventure or something about where it was to end. His cousin's smile seemed to tell him that he was being pressed forward into a world where his ultimate discoveries would be nothing other than the revealing of the principles without which nothing could even have begun. But there was nothing really for him to do with his insight. After all, he was in a taxi. Taxis go from point A to point B. They do not dissolve because of the illumination shed by a second-order insight.

As they rode along the rutted dirt road, Hans thought back to his childhood impression of Ricky as a bigger, stronger boy then he. Ricky was always the country boy to the suburban Hans. Then Hans recalled in embarrassed discomfort the occasions on which the two cousins had shared their most recent discoveries about their respective adolescent bodies. These conversations were terrifying to Hans. Ricky had told bragging, laughing tales of back-country "boys clubs" of masturbation and anal sex. This was not what Hans wanted to be thinking about at just this moment. He looked over at Ricky, furtively, half dreading that his cousin had somehow overheard his thoughts. He knew he was blushing. His cousin returned his gaze, then looked away, amused.

Hans had not seen much of his cousin since those earlier days. He dimly recalled going fishing once in their teens, staying in a trailer that had been dragged to some desolate Wisconsin lakeside. He recalled that while their fathers finished off bottles of beer in the fishing boat and bottles of vodka in the trailer, he was driven by an excitable Ricky in and out of dark pine groves in a large American car. A Buick, if he recalled. His cousin never seemed to have more than one hand on the wheel or one eye on the road. The only thing worse than those rides was actually having to take that fatal step back into the metal hulk, the rusting blue and white trailer, where their fathers soaked in a neutral grain brine. Hans particularly remembered the size of his uncle Don's plastic cup (some absurd Taco Joint 32-ounce thing with cartoon characters on the side, Yosemite Sam and the Tasmanian Devil, better suited for watering flowers than for drinking). Uncle Don would open a new bottle of cheap vodka from the supermarket and pour it into the cup right to the rim. He remembered his uncle sipping at the brimming cup and smiling like some lost little boy who didn't want to spill his milk. Within the hour, it would all be gone.

Hans pulled himself from these reveries. He remembered his aunt's charge to him: "Find out how Ricky is. Bring him home if you can." So Hans gave his cousin a once over and remarked, "Ricky, you look so well. Don't try to tell me that there is something wrong with you. You're strong as ever. There can't be anything so wrong that you couldn't come home with me."

"Return with you?" replied his cousin, really engaging his brown eyes with Hans's blue. Ricky's eyes were sad, sad to death, but there was also a keenness or, one might almost want to say, an avidity about them. "Cousin, you haven't yet had a chance to experience our Elixir. Wait a bit. You'll see. It's not so easy for those of us who were sent here to recover. I know to you I look healthy, but the truth is that I'm dangerously ill. I haven't been capable of leaving our little encampment in over a year. You are merely seeing and mistaking trivial consequences of my treatment."

"But you really do seem well."

"Seem," Ricky replied, nodding his head emphatically, nodding with both resignation and indifference, nodding as if he did it for the whole world, "one's ideas about seeming and being get changed up here. You'll hear all you'll ever need to hear about the differences between seeming and being. The Reverend Boyle will explain all that to you." He gazed at Hans apparently trying to imagine this encounter between his wet-behind-the-ears cousin and the august Reverend. "Phenues Boyle, Cousin. You'll see. Oh yes, by God, you will surely see," and he giggled at the idea.

Hans was, once again, perplexed by his cousin's comments. He didn't know if he had any general ideas about *seeming*. He didn't know if he *wanted* to have any ideas about seeming, especially if they came from someone named Phenues Boyle. Now *there* was a name! So he turned his attention out the taxi window to the spectacle that presented itself there.

"You're looking at the scenery?" asked Ricky.

"Yes. I've never spent much time in the country."

Ricky smiled. "That's right. You *are* the city cousin."

"This is very nice."

"Think so?"

"Sure. Don't you?"

"Depends on what you think of slag heaps."

"What's that?"

"Those."

"Those mountains?"

"They're hardly mountains, Cousin. They're leavings from old coal mines, and nothing grows on them except certain perversely ambitious weeds."

"What about all these little lakes we've passed. They're nice."

"Those are called 'borrow pits' that were dug out years ago when they built the interstate. And they would be nice if they hadn't also been accumulating . . . oh what shall I call it for your sake . . . stuff that trickles from the old mines." Ricky laughed one of his frequent, deep, and bitter laughs. "You can catch a fish in them, but you won't want to look at it. The fish in these ponds have had 'the change' worked on them, as we say. And no one is silly enough to eat them anymore. Not even these absurd local bumpkins who are the victims of their own 'change.' In the old days, these yokels might have lacked their teeth, but now there's no telling what they'll lack. Toes. Ears. The ability to breathe while walking. Or, worse yet, what they've gained!"

"Really. What do you mean by *stuff*?"

Ricky shrugged and rubbed his forehead between his eyes with a stiff index finger.

"Just stuff, Cousin. More of the same stuff." He paused. "Look, try not to ask so many questions. Questions only get in the way here."

Hans thought about his cousin's strange attitude.

"Don't you like nature, Ricky?"

Ricky looked as if, already, he were using the last of his patience with Hans. He took no pleasure in explaining what was obvious to him. "Look, old boy, I know you've spent the last four years in some sort of God-forsaken dormitory archipelago, and I suppose after that experience this vista might look good to anyone. Even for us, I admit, there are times when the place looks almost beautiful. When the rains come—if they come—and the corn looks very green and the air is clear and calm. We could almost forget that there are no trees, only crows and starlings for birds, and everything just a warped sameness. But trust me, Cousin, you get sick of looking at it. All of us here are disgusted and bored with it."

"My God, you have a strange way of talking now," said Hans.

"Have I?" Ricky smiled ruefully and pondered again how things look from another perspective, how *he* might look. He seemed to conclude something, then looked full into his cousin's eyes. "Tell me, how strange do I seem?"

Hans began stammering again in extreme discomfort, and Ricky laughed the frightening and annoying laughter of the addled and pretentious adolescent. For the first but not the last time, Hans wondered metaphysically, "How long is two weeks?"

After a moment's silence, Hans decided to risk another question. (He was, after all, here on a mission from his aunt, and he wasn't going to admit defeat already.)

"That's another thing that I don't understand. This 'we' business. It's confusing to me. Why do you keep referring to 'we,' as if your fate, your health, were somehow wrapped up with these others? I assume that you all came here separately, you have your own distinct conditions, and I hope you don't propose to stay here until you are all recovered. Can you explain this to me?"

Hans's question showed that there is room for bravery in abject terror.

"Oh, Cousin, you know, you have no ground for worry on that point. We are all separate in the end. They never bundle us together. Quite careful about that, they are. We lose several among our number every week. They're wrapped in green bags. Look like stuffed grape leaves, if you know what those are. It's an easy thing when the trains are running. But during the 'heavy' season, they have to ask farmers to take them out on tractors and sleds. In heavy weather, during times of tornadic snow, they'll sometimes pick the human bodies up right along with the frozen farm creatures, mostly pigs."

"Are you trying to say that they haul human bodies with tractors? Lord! That's a funny thing to imagine. And the pigs right with them?" Hans paused to contemplate this scene and its consequences. "Oh, you know, Ricky, you couldn't have that in a factory situation. No, no. That would have a very negative impact on the morale of the workers, believe me. Taking the dead workers out on dollies or skids to the loading dock? Never mind the frozen pigs. Oh, you'd have a very horrendous drop in productivity." Hans was giggling a little as he embellished this scene.

Now it was Ricky's turn to see his cousin as strange. "You have the funniest ideas, old boy. I'm overrun by them. You've taken your academic studies quite to heart, haven't you? You really care about 'drops in productivity.'"

"Of course. Everyone should. Who wants the economy to go to hell?"

"Oh, no one, obviously," said Ricky, seeming to ridicule someone or something, although Hans couldn't have said whom or what. "It's just that some things are not supportable by the facts. For instance, the way you keep things separate. We've forgotten how to do that up here. For us, for example, the factory and the country aren't really different."

"They're not?"

"No, of course not. The factory annihilated the country many years ago, before we were born, Cousin."

Hans was about to ask what Ricky could mean by annihilation when Ricky gestured silently to him as if to say "just a moment." Their taxi was nearly in front of The Elixir. Inexplicably, Ricky began screaming at the driver.

"You thieving piece of shit! Stop the car here before I get really angry! I've got a gun and believe me I would think nothing of using it! For me, blowing your head off would be a mercy to all the people around you who are sick of looking at your scabrous face! I know your kind! Stop the car! Get out! Get out and give us our fucking luggage!"

The driver did, rather calmly, as he was told. They all got out and as the man walked around to retrieve the suitcase from the passenger side, Hans whispered, "Ricky, why are you saying those awful things to this poor man?"

"Just watch and learn, Cousin."

The driver set the suitcase at Hans's feet.

"How much?" asked Ricky.

"Twelve-fifty."

Ricky handed him a ten and a five and the driver turned around, got back in the cab, and drove away.

Hans stood by his cousin, mouth agape. "Do you think you can explain that to me?"

"He was going to steal your things."

"How do you know that?"

"He has to. His comrades back at the train station will expect one of two things. Either he'll have your stolen things or he'll have a convincing story about how big my gun was. Without one of those two things, there's a very real chance that they'd simply drag him from the car and beat him to death for the disrespect he has brought on them. Or the burning necklace. That's a nice one that a South African driver brought to the local station several years ago. Fill a tire with gasoline, put it around the neck and set it ablaze. No one much cares so long as they keep their exotic practices to themselves. Quite a surprise to an Irish driver last year, though, poor devil."

"And then you gave him a tip!"

"Another little local custom. They'll put up with the threats and abuse, but if you don't give them a nice fat tip they'll be back with some real heavy artillery. Make my little gun seem like something made of licorice."

"A gun made of licorice! That's so funny," observed Hans. He paused very seriously. "But you don't really have a gun, do you? I mean a real gun."

"Oh, Cousin, I *have* a gun. And they bloody well know it from hard experience." Ricky raised his shirt to reveal the flat plank-like muscles of his stomach and, against it, an enormous revolver stuck into his pants. "Don't worry. I've got an extra that you can use during your stay."

"But I don't want a gun."

At that point Ricky seemed to cross some unknowable but deeply carved psychological boundary. In his own mind, he had been very patient with his cousin. But, clearly, he wanted to emphasize something. Ricky took his cousin by the collar and said, "While you are here, old boy, you will carry a fucking revolver." Ricky looked as if he could eat him.

Hans stared at his cousin. Abruptly, Ricky laughed, put his arm around Hans's shoulder and led him toward The Elixir saying, "Relax. If you're worried about it going off in your pants, I've got a shoulder holster you can borrow."

Alas, poor Hans Castorp. The experiences are coming on him with a bewildering speed. He begins to shape a new insight into one of his textbook concepts—"personality meltdown." He begins to suspect that the not-so-elaborate construct of his own personality could "melt down." His Hans Castorp-ness could puddle at his feet. For what is Hans Castorp? What qualities are his? What is proper to him? What is his own? How does he maintain his peculiar "suchness" in relation to others? Well, he was a student. He has studied X content for four years. That study has given him some "content," too, one can be sure. But a train ride which has taken him through fields of corn, in among mountains of pulsing coal trailing, here into this Valley of Recovery, has made all Castorp-qualities strangely vulnerable, fragile, and friable. Hans feels composed only of tiny oscillating bits likely to fly off at any moment. Nothing he "knows" helps him to speak to his cousin Ricky. His encounter with Ricky is like an encounter with an alien life form. He is collapsing. He is being saturated by something other. A new world penetrates him, pushing old qualities before it until it reaches his core, at which point Hans will be annihilated!

It's a good thing that Hans finished his last exams before coming here.

$2)$

"Well, this is it," said Ricky, gesturing broadly, "what do you think?"

Hans thought he had never seen anything quite like it. The Elixir was simply a series of buildings lined up along the north side of a very narrow country road. A health facility, he had imagined, would be full of large shady trees and lots of softening landscape. There should be broad lawns on which families might picnic with the ailing. He expected such a place to appeal to the timeless calm of nature. He expected reassuring brick bungalows reminiscent of WPA-style social stability. But these buildings communicated something very different. They said: we have nothing in common with each other. We are here because we are unwanted anywhere else in the world. Starting from the right, the east, there was a rusting Quonset hut that served as a meeting area and movie hall. (Hans had never seen one before except in some old movies about World War II. He could never look at Quonset huts without expecting prop-driven airplanes to come out of them.) Next there was what appeared to be an abandoned fast-food franchise. It was of indeterminate denomination; most of the corporate markings had been messily obliterated. Then there was a squat, brick bank building with the legend "Farmers Bank of

Pontiac—1886" still boldly carved in the limestone above its door. Then a Victorian-era farm house, stripped of all detail and covered in dented aluminum siding. Old peeling white paint dangled from it like party decorations. A Spee-D-Lube, a 7-11 medical center, and then an abandoned Mr. Donut with all corporate markings still perfectly visible. Finally, a grain elevator into which crude windows had been cut, creating a very primitive-looking high-rise apartment complex.

Hans stood before this vision in awe. It looked at one moment familiar—it was a strip mall!—and at the next spookily strange— alien spacecraft had transported these buildings here using powerful tractor beams! It was so much free-floating space junk. No one piece of junk had any relation to the next, let alone to the environment created by the mountains of coal trailings looming behind. These buildings seemed simply enormous, unmoored and dangerous.

It was at that moment that Hans noticed something else. It was a smell. The smell came on the wind. It was a plainly stinking wind. It colored everything he saw. Hans tried to figure what this wind smelled like since it didn't smell like any wind he'd ever smelled before (although it can't be said he'd smelled that many winds in his Downstate University dormitory). He finally concluded that the wind smelled like someone was boiling tennis balls.

"You'll be staying in the Mr. Donut," said Ricky, interrupting Hans's first impressions. He pulled a flask from inside his jacket. "Cheers!" he offered, tipping the flask back and taking a measured swallow.

Hans didn't know what presented the most immediate threat, the Mr. Donut, this unbelievable stinking, or Ricky's flask. All of them alarmed him. He turned back to the Mr. Donut. It seemed to loom before him, beckoning, winking, shifting its obscene pastry thighs. He considered what it would mean to submerge himself in this donut home. His panicky mantra again intruded: "How long is two weeks?"

Back to his cousin.

"Ricky, what in the world is that smell?"

Ricky looked at his cousin in surprise. "Good lord, don't tell me that you can still smell it."

"Smell what?"

"You said that you smelled something."

"Yes, but I don't know what it is."

"Well, what else could it be?"

"What are you thinking it could be?"

"Well, the Big Stinking, of course."

"I have no idea what that is."

"It was a mammoth disaster. A Stinking Event of the first magnitude. A smell so bad it actually registered on the Richter scale. A shocking smell."

"Oh."

"But, it was so long ago. I assumed it was all gone. I guess that we're just used to it. It was reported at the time to be a very changeable smell. Most often it was likened to the smell of boiling tennis balls."

"That's amazing. That's just the idea that I had of it."

"Well, don't worry about it too much. It's not dangerous. It's just a smell. A lingering smell of a very long ago incident that we don't really like to remember."

"Why?"

"Because it smelled bad."

Hans concluded that he wouldn't get any further with this line of questioning. "And Ricky, don't think I didn't notice. What are you drinking there?" asked Hans.

"Cognac, old boy. VSOP."

"I meant *why* are you drinking? I meant, you are *drinking*. I thought you were sent here precisely because of your drinking." This let the cat out of his aunt's bag to a degree.

"Easy, Cousin," Ricky replied, replacing the cap on his flask with theatrical aplomb. "Three things: first, I don't know who told you this—my mother no doubt." He looked Hans dead in the eye. "My mother has no right to an opinion about my drinking. She has her own past and her own conduct to account for. I won't say any more on that subject. Second, in my opinion, drinking is involved but not constitutive in my condition. Necessary but not sufficient, as they say. My illness is not something that can be labeled so simply. Finally, for your own part, take the time to get to know the place before you start making judgments. This is not your world. Thank God. If I lived in your world, I'd feel like I'd placed my head in a fucking Band-Aid box. And shut the lid! We have our own ways here."

Hans tried to keep up with Ricky's rapidly progressing assumptions.

"Well, I may not know much about this place yet, but it's very confusing, Ricky. And what do you mean 'in your opinion' your drinking is not constitutive? What about your doctor's opinion? What does that count for?"

Ricky spread one of his sly, knowing smiles between the two of them. "My doctor has recused himself from my case."

"Recused?"

"Yes. Conflict of interest, so to speak. But enough chatting. Let me show you your room."

They went through the Mr. Donut's front door as if it were Sunday morning and they wanted something glazed, then through the hinged gap in the counter where thousands of waitresses immemorial had passed before. Hans thought he could still smell the fat, the burning coffee, and the cigarettes. There were, however, no actual donuts in the display case. Towels, toiletries and cleansers were stacked neatly in their place.

Passing through the door that once led to the kitchen, Hans found himself in a clean, well-appointed living space complete with a tiny alcove for preparing meals. It was even nicer than his dorm room. For the first time since stepping down out of the train, he felt the hope that a degree of comfort and security was not out of the question here.

Ricky stood at Hans's elbow frankly evaluating his reaction. "You're lucky to have this room, you know. I didn't think it would become available in time. It is the premier guestroom in the complex. You'll enjoy total privacy here. I'd feared you might have to take one of those uncomfortable little cells behind the tellers' booth in the old Farmer's Bank. Or in the grain elevator, good God!"

"I'm glad for that. But what happened to this room's last occupant? Not taken off in one of your sleds, I hope."

"In fact they used the station wagon since the weather was good. You might have seen it pull up to the luggage car as you got off the train. But you had other things on your mind, eh?

"A fascinating woman, though. She and her sister, as teenagers, had become convinced, through some sort of elaborate juvenile fantasy, that the only way to ensure the further populating of the world was by having children through their own father. So they would intoxicate their father (and themselves while they were at it) and then, essentially, rape him. The oldest daughter died at seventeen. The father checks in and out of here like the coming and going of seasons. The second, younger daughter was in here for years."

"And did they in fact have children?"

Ricky reached again into his jacket for his flask. He took a hit. "Oh, one or two. You'll see them. They're here. No biggee."

Hans thought he had learned as much about the previous occupant as he needed to know. For no good reason, he nervously opened a desk drawer, against which he had been leaning. There he saw a wad of Kleenex with a clot of hair wrapped within it, a pencil, and an open tube of lipstick on which it appeared something had been gnawing. He shut the drawer. "Well, this is really a very decent room. I think I can spend a couple of weeks here with great pleasure."

"That's the spirit. I'm glad you like it, old boy. As I say, its availability has a tragic side, but that is as it must be in this vale of tears, eh?" Ricky paused. "But I should tell you one more thing. The little boys who were the children to this woman have been coming to cry in the lobby area out front. In the days following their mother's death, they would sit out there all day long. They made quite a racket. They'd cry until their cheeks chapped and stung from the salty tears, and then they'd rub their mother's cold cream into each other's face. They weren't very subtle about it. The cream got mixed in with the tears, and they had no sense of how much cold cream was really needed. After a while, their faces looked like they'd been meringued."

"That's really sad."

"Yes, I suppose it is, now that you mention it. But we also suspect that they were drinking from their mother's stash of vodka."

"No! The children?"

"At any rate, they probably won't be back since their mother has been carted off. But they might return looking for the vodka." Ricky looked sternly at his cousin. "Now, old boy, if the children return you tell them this: 'Your mother is dead. There is nothing for you here. I will not give you any juice. Go away.'"

Hans thought about this with a pained expression on his face. "Isn't that sort of hard on them? They're just children, I guess."

Ricky pushed his face into his cousin's. "Get this, Hans. It will take these kids exactly three days to drain you of your life if you make the mistake of sympathizing with them. Tell them to get the bloody hell fucking away from you. That's all."

"Well, maybe you're right. The place is in good order now and I should try to keep it that way. Children are messy. Except that smell."

"Another smell?"

"Yes, I smell something. It smells like . . . donuts!" Suddenly a strange, unnatural hilarity got the better of him. He laughed out loud. He could not stop. He laughed so hard the tears came down his cheeks. He rocked with laughter. He put his hands to his face. He thought he could feel cold cream there. He mixed it up. He meringued it.

"You know, Cousin," said Ricky, distanced from Hans's mirth, "you may fit in here much better than I ever expected."

Thus it was that Hans was introduced to the hole at the heart of him.

3)

After Hans had been shown his room, Ricky led him back down
the street, past the Farmer's Bank of Pontiac and the Spee-D-Lube,
to the fast-food franchise of uncertain denomination. Hans felt, as
anyone might, alien. But the gun that his cousin had shoved into
his back pocket made his estrangement worse. The revolver felt like
it was a knuckle of bone that had been removed from his body and
reapplied to his exterior. It felt awkward in that way that something
meant for the inside but applied to the outside must feel awkward.

As they entered, Hans tried to guess the original denomination of
the establishment. "Ah, it is chicken, isn't it? But not KFC. Right?"

"You're on the mark as usual, Cousin."

Hans beamed. "Oh, I know. It's a Daffy's. Daffy Duck's Chicken.
One of the smaller franchises. And dumber. Duck chicken! Went
belly-up not long ago. I remember reading about it in a book on the
psycho-social dynamics of the fast-food industry. Daffy's deliberately
sought out single-parent women for their workforce on the theory
that they would be more desperate and compliant than KFC's and
McDonald's high-school kids. That was their corporate gambit in
the time of the fast-food wars. They secretly supplied these women

with amphetamines. Just to make sure. Boy, they felt great. Like they were nine-year-olds. And then one spring, these gaunt, strung-out women gathered in Washington, D.C., for the great Duck Walk for Fast-Food Justice. Pathetic, really. Last straw for the corporation, too. Daffy's declared bankruptcy *while* its five thousand employees were standing in the Great Mall, shivering before Lincoln's Monument, skeletal from years of adrenal abuse, their hair pulled back in the oily buns fashionable among speed freaks. By the time they returned to their respective towns, the buildings themselves had either been leveled or pulled up and hauled away. And here's one of them. It's very interesting, Cousin. We stand inside history. And, oh look!, there's a silhouette of Daffy himself." He pointed to a window where adhesive had etched the ghost of Daffy Duck into the glass.

Ricky nodded vaguely.

"Say," Hans considered, "we're not going to have to eat chicken all the time, are we?"

"Truthfully, Hans, it's not always clear to me what the food here 'is.' But we like it. It is enough for us." Ricky nodded proudly.

Like most fast-food franchises, this building was gaudily furnished. It was lit by long, exposed fluorescent tubes that hung from recesses above the cheap acoustic ceiling tiles. A large number of tiles were missing, exposing the mechanics of the building. The orange and red tables and chairs were all faded and chipped plastic.

Ricky commented that this was often a happy spot where the premium American lager flowed and the conversation was lively. "We have a sense of family here, Cousin. We're family of choice."

This sounded very pleasant to Hans. And he was getting hungry. A good sign. He spread several paper napkins in his lap. Suddenly, with a rush of tumultuous screaming and laughter, a crowd of children ran out from the kitchen area with warm paper bags that they deposited on the table. Just as quickly, with just as many loud screams and giggles, they disappeared back behind the swinging kitchen doors.

"What did we order?" asked Hans, his mood lifting as he opened one of the toasty bags.

Ricky smirked, a little condescendingly. A lock of brownish-blond hair fell across his brow. He looked stunningly northern. "As you know, Cousin, we didn't order anything. We're getting what we get." He frowned. "Look," he said with irritation, "you're being granted a generosity here. You don't see any other's enjoying this early meal, do you?"

Hans blushed and stammered, horrified that he may have seemed ungrateful. "I'm sorry. I don't mean to seem arrogant. I'll happily eat whatever I'm served."

Hans then opened one of the bags, a Burger King bag, and peered inside. It was full of small plastic containers of ketchup, mustard and mayonnaise, a few of them burst, which the kitchen urchins had apparently microwaved and for no short period.

"Ricky, this bag is full of hot condiments."

Ricky sighed and looked toward the ceiling. It was as if he knew that yet another not-refusable obligation was about to be his. A textbook concept came to Hans: the so-called "Misery of Mastery." He'd aced that class. "Social Construction and Imposition of Mastery in American Industry." Not simple stuff either. Very advanced management theory. For the first time it occurred to Hans that Ricky—forceful and determined though he might seem—was under a lot of stress. Like the over-burdened CEOs Hans had studied, Ricky was a force of gravity holding a whole world together, but it was a world whose most natural desire was to fly apart. Hans wanted to sympathize, but he wanted to sympathize from a safe distance.

Ricky opened another of the bags, this one with a Jack-in-the-Box logo, and looked inside. French fry bags full of pickle chips charbroiled to a fineness. "I think," he surmised, "that we may have a degree of childish resentment working here. I suppose that they don't like having to feed people at the wrong time. I'll take care of it." He gathered up the bags and strode back toward the kitchen.

Hans feared that the children would be punished for their prank. He felt a little guilty about this since, as he'd already learned, The Elixir was hardly an ideal environment for children. He braced himself for unpleasant shouting or a loud banging. Maybe a slap. But he heard nothing. After what was perhaps ten minutes of silence, he did at last hear a muffled voice growing steadily louder, beginning at first as a chilling moan, and peaking finally in a persistent complaint. "Ow-oweee!"

A few minutes later, Ricky returned with two Styrofoam plates heaped with warm food. The plate Ricky placed before Hans contained three chicken nugget type things, the bottom half of a hamburger bun, a dozen or so small dark French fries (someone had obviously tried to re-heat already cooked French fries by placing them back in the fry vat), some of the steaming pickles from Ricky's earlier bag, some shredded lettuce airily here and there, and finally somewhere deep beneath it all a sort of bedrock of what appeared to be a pancake. There was also a small carton of milk that Ricky produced from his coat pocket. It was warm, already opened, and maybe a little more than half-full.

Hans looked up from his meal in amazement.

Ricky returned his look with one of irritation. "That's what I could find." Pause. "It's not always like this." Pause. "Okay you don't want this shit, you don't have to eat it."

Reaching across the table, Ricky grabbed the plates violently, French fries and chicken nuggets spilling off, and carried them over to an already over-flowing trash bin. He stuffed the plates in, and about half of the food fell to the floor. He then walked back to the kitchen—this time the children really did scream—but returned quickly with a six-pack of beer. He was obviously finding it difficult to control himself. "Fucking babies," he concluded. Hans wondered if he were included in this judgment. He popped a can of the beer and drained half of the first one in a single draught. "Don't be shy, Cousin, help yourself."

Hans didn't want a beer, but he didn't know how to say no to his cousin. Ricky stared at Hans, polished off his first beer, and said, "Okay, then, Cousin Emissary. You-who-will-do-my-mommy's-bid-ding. You-who-will-do-her-bidding-by-doing-nothing-other-than-gawk-with-a-half-baked-expression-on-your-face, as if you'd never seen a person drink a beer before. Why don't you just go back to your room? The real dinner is only a few hours off." He smiled grimly. "Then you can eat something more substantial."

"Okay," agreed Hans, "I'll see you later."

4)

Hans stood. He meant to turn, walk away, and return to his quiet
quarters. Inexplicably, he saw himself reach for one of the beers, tug it
with difficulty from its polystyrene ring, open it and take a long drink.
A curious restlessness, at once pleasurable and annoying, overtook his
limbs. It felt like energy, but not energy he was in control of. He tried
to say something, but his words fell all over each other. So he tried to
gesture but the gesture seemed magically to acquire significance not
even he could imagine. So, he shrugged his shoulders.

His cousin stared at him stonily. Hans choked his can of beer.
Ricky decided to speak.

"Have you ever had this experience, Cousin? You're crossing a
street, preoccupied with some petty matter. You bounced a check,
or yet another uncle died somewhere. Something like that. A car is
coming. You wait for it to pass. It passes at a velocity that makes it
clear that it is indifferent to your health. You begin to cross in its
just vacated path. Halfway through, it occurs to you with a real jolt,
'Did I remember to let the car pass?' You look up in panic. Then
you ask yourself a related but different question, how can I be sure I
would see the car even if it were there? Crossing a busy street is not

a good time for a meditation on how our sense perception deceives us, Cousin. Well, funny though it may seem to you (and it does have its comic side), this sort of experience is a constant state of Mind here at The Elixir. Having a cup of tea in that psychic landscape is not so restful, old boy. That's where these come in handy." He patted what remained of his six-pack as if it were the sturdy head of a faithful Labrador. "You know, some people, even some people in that other world you call home, understand that each year they pass over the date of their eventual death. On one day each year you are stepping on your own grave without knowing it. Does your little dormitory head understand this? Here at The Elixir, though, this understanding is so well established that merely waking up in the morning feels like playing Russian Roulette." He looked at Hans through narrowed eyes upon which nothing was lost. "Say, Cousin, have you ever considered the uncertainty of the hour of your own death?"

Ricky waited only a moment for Hans's response before concluding, "Yes, we sit here and laugh, but this place is not funny. It's not funny at all, Cousin."

Hans was bewildered by Ricky's talk, but he was most bewildered by his allusion to laughter, of which there had been exactly none.

"But we persevere. We keep moving ahead." Ricky took a meditative swallow from his beer. "It's the good fight, isn't it, Cousin?"

Hans had no idea what he was talking about. So he set his beer on the table, still nearly full in spite of his attempts at swallowing, and walked out without a word of goodbye.

He was by himself for the first time. The painful strangeness of this place pressed him. Here again was the strip mall of displaced space junk. And there was that stinking wind again. This time, though, it wasn't boiling tennis balls. It smelled now more like plastic beach thongs being simmered in chicken fat.

A short distance from the restaurant, he saw a little boy sitting on a blue, plastic milk crate. He was very unhappy about something. His little face was buried in his hands. For a moment Hans wondered, a little weirdly, if this child weren't somehow related to Ricky's story about walking in front of passing cars. He wondered if perhaps this child might not be something dangerous that he should allow to pass by. The best response might be to walk quickly on pretending not to notice him. But, then, Hans had already noticed. He couldn't deny it. He was the kind of person who noticed things. Like the back of the boy's shirt. There were four streaks of drying blood on this boy's white shirt, as if someone had wiped fingers down his back. The boy looked up at the sound of Hans's footsteps, and Hans saw that it was one of the children who had "served" him.

"What's the matter, little fellow?" asked Hans, oddly self-conscious of his gesture. "Why are you crying?"

The boy wiped at his snotty face with the back of his pudgy hand and complained, "Mister Ricky hurt me."

Hans was now bent down beside the boy, talking to him "at his own level." He indulged this gesture of concern. "Oh well, you know, he was just a little upset that you played a trick on us."

"Oh big deal!" he cried out. "Big deal! Why was giving you hot ketchup and stuff so bad? We thought it was funny."

"Well, I'm new here, you know, and he was probably hoping to make a good impression. I'm sure he didn't mean to hurt you."

"No, he hurt me bad," the boy whined, outraged at Hans skepticism, stretching the words out as children who imagine great injury do.

Hans frowned. "Okay, tell me where it hurts."

"He hurt my bottom."

"Your bottom. You mean he spanked you."

"I'm bleeding for crissakes!" the boy screamed.

Hans thought again of the bloody marks on his little back.

"What's your name, little fellow?"

"Teddy. And I'm not your little fellow. Where are you supposed to be from? You talk funny." He buried his face in his crossed arms.

"Teddy. Nice to meet you. I'm Hans."

Teddy looked up. "And you got a funny name, too. What kinda name is that? Hans. Like hands?"

"It's a regular name, I think."

"You gotta be kiddin'. That's a stupid name. I sure never heard it before."

"Well, I'm glad to meet you." He extended his hand.

"Sure. Okay. Me too," replied Teddy. He did not extend his own hand.

"Tell me, Teddy, where do you live?"

"Well, I used to stay in the Mr. Donut with my mommy, but she's dead. They put her on the tractor."

Guilt rinsed over Hans. But something in him resisted the guilt. And why not? It wasn't his idea to throw out the orphans to make room for him. What was he supposed to do? Sleep in a field for two weeks? Perhaps it was these thoughts that led him to try to correct what he thought was a factual error in Teddy's comment. "You mean, I think, that they put her in a station wagon. I believe that they only use the tractor and sled in heavy winter. Right? When the snow tornadoes come through?"

Teddy looked at Hans as if he were an idiot and a cruel idiot at that.

"What station wagon, mister? They took my mommy on the regular tractor. The one that comes through every day. She's my mommy, I saw it, and I know." He stood up from his milk crate as if to emphasize his point.

"I'm sorry. Calm down. Perhaps I'm mistaken."

"I'll say you are. You ought to know what you're talking about before you start talking."

Hans tried to return to a caring posture. "So where do you stay now?"

"They let me stay in the restaurant to work for as many hours as I like. Except when I'm bad like today when I gave you the bag of hot condominiums or whatever you call them. Then I have to go outside. But since I've been bad, I deserve it."

Hans sensed something very sad in this admission. He didn't know quite how to put it. "Well, Teddy, I don't know much about it, but I think that you have a right to be sad. Not having a home is very sad." Hans recognized his words before they were even out of his mouth. It was his instructor in Dysfunctional Family Counseling I. The hands-on stuff. The daily reflections framed on the wall. The therapeutic aromas. Professor Thomas Bardo. His whole point seemed to be that it was great to think that everyone had a right to be sad. Bardo—a guy with a ponytail and open-neck, organic, cotton Deva shirt—seemed to positively glory in everyone's sadness.

But Teddy wasn't buying it. He looked at Hans with a startling clarity. "Who said anything about being sad?" He scowled. "Oh, God. You're not one of those, are you?"

"One of what?"

"One of those 'bleeding hearts' that Reverend Boyle tells us about."

As I've said, Hans was not a greatly experienced young man. He was born and stuck in a vinyl box, and before he was conscious he was put in school, and he stayed there until school spit him back out. He knew nothing about what Teddy called "bleeding hearts."

Teddy stretched to his full chubby length to make his next point. "The things you hear about the homeless"—and Hans had in truth heard next to nothing about the homeless—"are lies. The newspapers say that corporations don't care about us and that's why people are living on the street. Ha!" Teddy bounced his little belly and stood high on his sturdy legs. Already Hans backed away from the pudgy prodigy. "They're living on the street for one reason: they're stupid! They make stupid choices like . . . choosing to live on the street!"

Teddy laughed and spun around, the blood on the back of his shirt flashing. He crowed in the exuberance of his mastery of this knowledge.

"The homeless are the result of a lack of personal responsibility and a generation-long decline in respect for the traditional American values of hard work! As if you'd know anything about hard work."

Hans was walking rapidly away from the boy. But Teddy wasn't done. He gave chase. "You're not getting away so easy as that, Mr. Sensitive-Soul-Who-Does-Nothing-to-Solve-the-Problem. You feel 'sorry' for me? Does that help you to feel good? Why don't you take responsibility? Are you inviting me to share your Mr. Donut bed to-night?" Teddy gave a lewd wink that Hans just saw looking back over his shoulder. "I think you would keep a little boy warm, eh? Not so warm as my mommy used to keep me, but warm enough. And why don't you get a job? How come you're not working? This some sort of travel holiday hot-spot for you? Hey, come back here! What's up? I'll chew on your leg!"

Hans had managed to run a little way ahead. He could just hear Teddy's last warning. "I'll be watching you now, Mr. Liberal. We know what to do with your type around here."

5

The Reverend Phenues Boyle, to whom Ricky has alluded ominously, was one of four points on The Elixir's spiritual compass. These four points kept mostly separate from each other, as if by magnetic repulsion. The Reverend Boyle was a force of orthodoxy. His influence was both supported and challenged by Ricky's vaguely militaristic rigor. Ricky, for his part, was a force of personal will. The two were almost never seen together for very fear of the consequences. The other two points on The Elixir's spiritual compass were taken by characters to whom we have not yet been introduced: Mayor Jesse (who embodied The Elixir's notion of administration and the rule of law), and one Professor Feeling (who, unlike the Mayor, respected only intuition and invention, although even his understanding of those two qualities was intuitive and inventive and therefore indistinguishable from bizarre). The Professor was never to be seen with either the Mayor or the Reverend because he interacted with their types like chlorine interacts with ammonia: it produces a choking and toxic gas. Hans will be introduced to all of these characters in due time.

How the Reverend Boyle maintained his spiritual influence is difficult to say. He was almost never seen on The Elixir campus. Legend had it that he had nailed his own feet to a platform out beyond the twin slag heaps called the Desiccated Sisters. But every so often, the Reverend would accompany Mayor Jesse on visits to residents during evening meditation. When he did so, he would distribute "discourses" in pamphlet form, one of which I now provide.

The Right Reverend Phenues Boyle Discourses on Family Ritual

Just as it is with Nations, a Family exists, has an identity of its own because of fundamental beliefs and attitudes which all members of the family share. This "sharing" must be rigorously policed and those who fail to share or who suggest sharing beliefs other than the original and True beliefs which have been passed down from generation to generation must be asked to leave the family. They must be either "put away" or "shut up."

So it is this Power within the family, that which allows it to survey and police its important and enduring domain—or its "dynasty"—that must first be stabilized. Because the figure of the Father is most comfortable with the role of enforcer of shared beliefs, because his character can best withstand the oft-times awesome distorting pressures of his role, and because he is not subject to "emotional incontinence" like the otherwise worthy figure of the Mother, it is to Him that the prerogatives (and, yes, the perquisites) of power have evolved.

In order to fulfill his function as enforcer of shared family attitudes, the Father must be privileged with certain "poses" which are in fact the instruments of his authority and which are awesome, imposing and, in the wrong hands, dangerous. First and foremost, the Father must have the right to silence. He must have the right to seem to exist at an icy remove, as if he owned the patent and was the sole proprietor of solitude. From this solitude he must, secondly, have the right to burst forth in righteous anger and pronounce fiats and dictums like, "Okay, that's it, I've warned you kids, now you're going to get it." He also has the right to indifference to the pain his anger causes. He has the right, thirdly, to speak without regret. He has the right to keep all of his "I'm sorries" to himself.

But this is a terrible burden. This burden creates a subset of Fatherly tolerances (that is, what we tolerate—indeed, welcome—*in* the Father) which help to mitigate the hardship of his functions. Hence, the father may have the first piece of chocolate fudge and this candy is always to be at his hand. He has the right to the full-length lounging on the couch while his children sprawl on the floor. He has the right to change the channel on the television set at his whim, a right given sudden and near-miraculous clarity by the so-called television "remote."

The Father has the right to fart, and fart most noisily. The family has the obligation to smell the fart but not to notice. (For to note that the Father farts, and in particular to protest said noting, is a heinous act subversive *in extremis*.) Let this "imago" speak metaphorically of the full degree and mythic extent of Fatherly prerogative.

Now I would like to address a highly theoretical issue that is speculative in the most ornate sense. The question has been asked, "Is the Father not merely the happenstansical 'Daddy' of given family X, but rather a superior (one wants almost to say 'calming') metaphor for legitimate authority in general? Could we not imagine, therefore, that the role of the Father could as easily fall upon the Mother, son or even daughter?"

I do not know who has asked this question, but it contains a serious, even dangerous, suggestion. Whoever it was should have thought about what he or she was saying, should have considered more carefully the consequences of a loosed Idea. For I have in fact now heard of speculative circumstances (that I can only call perverse) in which a daughter has performed the role of Father. This tale has come to me in the following form.

One of the great tolerances allowed the Father is his right to "booze." As a theoretical matter, the Father may "booze it up" whenever he chooses. In an instance I have heard of, a father who had exceeded his own biological tolerance for booze (who took the theoretically infinite social tolerance for booze too literally) actually fell from his couch. The horrified family was legitimately anxious to know how to proceed. Who, for example, would select the evening's television programming? I am informed that (in a moment I can only describe as horrifying) the daughter seized the opportunity, leapt over the fallen body of her father and assumed his august reclining posture on the couch. Now, the rest of the family might swiftly have torn her from the position citing chapter and verse (viz., "Uh-uh, you can't sit there, that's Daddy's chair"), but, looking her kin sternly in the eye, she is said to have farted both noisily and smellily thus assuring that her audacious coup would triumph for the period of her father's incapacity. I am further told that the lighter, sweeter smell of her effluvia caused some family members to become ill, and the mother, in particular, to remember troubling childhood events. Finally, I am assured that she used her brief flirtation with responsibility most irresponsibly by switching at whim between cartoons, home shopping, MTV, and nature programming for a period of days that are now known in family legend as "Dad's big doozy."

My point would be simply that this episode is dubious in its factuality, and that it would be a grave error to turn its sour *exemplum* into a theoretical endorsement of the implied concept: that daughters may function as Fathers. For this is a defilement and an abomination.

6)

Hans hoped he would feel better once he was back in his quarters. He thought he'd try reading a book. He'd seen some on the stand next to the bed. But once there and alone, the strangeness of Teddy's words made an already alien environment seem inter-stellar. Hans felt like he'd caught the sleeve of his jacket on the jagged edge of a distant star.

Hans got into bed. He thought he'd just take a nap until dinner. Much to his surprise, he did fall asleep, but he was startled immediately wide awake by this thought: just a few short days ago, a woman who had raped her drunken father and bore his child had died in this very bed. Hans imagined that he felt the bed sinking as if it were a casket being lowered into the ground. He turned on the bedside lamp to light the windowless room. He picked up a book on the bedside table. He smiled a strange, sad smile when he saw that it was a nice, fat novel. What else would one read in such a spa? One needed them for the long disturbing nights. This one was by a German writer, Thomas Mann. *The Magic Mountain*. Hans read for a while, skipping about. The experience was disappointing. Perhaps he was missing something, but the writer seemed to be telling a story in which the central dramatic incident was borrowing a pencil. One boy borrowed a pencil from another boy and then thought about it for the rest of his life. Couldn't forget it. To be fair, the description of the pencil made it seem like a very special pencil. A silver pencil holder with a ring in the end, which one screwed in order to make the pencil lead come out. A "simple mechanism." Hans couldn't quite figure it, though. Was telling such a story idiotic or charming? He both longed for novels and thought the world would be well-off without them. It was funny that this book made him think both thoughts at the same time.

Hans read on for a few more minutes and had just started to doze off again, bored by the writer's slow pace, when he noticed that there was something strange about the book. He was reading the phrase, "the agreeable sensation of being totally lost and abandoned," when he felt a "softness" in the book's center. If he pressed in the middle of the page, the book sprang back, like pressing the "soft spot" on an infant's head. He turned curiously toward the center of the book and, ouch!, a half-pint of vodka fell out and banged against his sternum.

Hans was stunned. What had he discovered? Was this the bottle of the woman who had lived here before him? If so, why hadn't she opened it? But then another possibility occurred to him. Had this bottle been placed here by the management specifically for him? One fact made him think so. This was a bottle of the cheapest imaginable grocery store vodka, Golden Gate vodka. And he remembered clearly from his childhood: it was his father's brand!

7)

Hans Castorp really understood next to nothing about his own parents. What kind of people were they? He didn't know. What were the times and places of their lives really like, and how had they shaped his mother and father? Frankly, he wouldn't even know how to begin to frame these questions let alone their answers. He always felt a curious numbing sensation when he tried to think, however vaguely, about his parents. Somehow, this numbness had led him to conclude that he didn't really have parents.

His mother was a farm girl from Ohio. Hans had never met her parents, his grandparents. It almost seemed as if he were expected to imagine that she, too, was one of those people who didn't have parents. It was a strangely easy thing for her to believe as well. When her parents, especially her father, was mentioned, her face would get tense, her brow furrow, and she would say simply, "I don't know anything about it," as if her parents were a subject she'd missed in school. When his mother said this, little Hans would think to himself that she was like a magical, black, hard-shelled beetle. Its magic was that it contained this hot energy which, if you opened the bug shell, would be like the sun.

Hans's father was not much different. He grew up on a farm in Georgia. He was the sixth child of a tense marriage between a restrictive and distant mother and a father given only to selling things (which was tolerated by his wife but which he was not particularly good at) and dancing (which was not tolerated by his wife but which he was quite good at). Eventually, he ran off with "another woman" who was more supportive of his desire to dance and less adamant about his selling things.

Hans's parents met through circumstances that must remain hopelessly vague for us because they've never made any sense to Hans. When he was very young, before the numbness, he believed they met in northern Idaho. He believed they were camping. He believed this because when he tried to think of their meeting, he saw sleeping bags. Old musty green cotton sleeping bags with red plaid interiors. He saw them sleeping side-by-side in the sleeping bags on beds of fragrant pine needles. The morning light was soft and clean and the air was fragrant. It was a happy but completely fabricated memory. Nonetheless, he clung to it until that day, which we will come to, when anything like memory was driven from his mind.

Whatever the truth, Hans's family began in a kind of blithe optimism and confidence that professor Bardo would have called "lacking in self-knowledge." They moved to a "suburb" of the Quad Cities and lived in a vinyl-clad nightmare. His father's first job was with a janitorial supply company. He was a "disinfectant technician." Hans had no idea what a disinfectant technician was, so he had no idea what his father did. Sometimes it seemed to him important and proud work. At other times, in the "disappointing later," he could only imagine his despairing father sitting in a cubicle and receiving box after box of dirty, broken things. He received boxes of broken glass. He would sift through the tiny pieces with scarred and bleeding fingers, taking bits out and trying to clean them. He smoked and wept down into the boxes where his tears and the smoke from his cigarettes fused the fragments into grotesque animal shapes. In Hans's most powerful memory of his father (but it was not a "memory" at all; it was a dream emerging from a wound) his father was sitting at the tiny dining room table in their vinyl home wearing his business suit. His fingers were laced with the thousands of tiny cuts he received at his work. He was smoking and drinking Golden Gate vodka from a little gimlet glass. He was trying to explain why he couldn't touch anything, especially his son. Blood got on the things that he touched. He didn't want to make a mess. He didn't want to get blood on his son. The scars were so thick that he could feel nothing, so there was really no touch to his touching. The only sensation in touching was the pain from the glass cuts and splinters. He reached into his pocket and pulled out one of the bizarre glass abominations. They seemed to be everywhere around the house as if they were little creatures, trolls and gremlins, who thought this house was really their own. His fingers must have caught on a sharp edge because immediately his fingertips began bleeding. The blood dripped down the side of the glass creature and the whole thing began resonating in a rich rose. It was both beautiful and sinister. It was a barnacle. It was a tumor. It was an eternal flower encased in ice.

Finally—and these were the last words Hans remembered from his father, in spite of the fact that he was not dead—Mr. Castorp said, "What is this thing? I know I made it. But what is it? Can anyone help me?"

It should be clear that I mean to say what is true and relevant of Hans's youth. He was neither entirely hero nor victim. His response to his first home was neither brilliant nor stupid. In short, he coped and in coping he was shaped. But there is evidence that he was capable of figuring things out. Once, his big sister was away for a summer and when he wrote to her he found himself asking questions, questions in which he surprised and scared himself.

". . . and so if Daddy left us and went away somewhere, wouldn't he just be one of those homeless bums? Like a hobo type of guy? He already only wears one pair of pants. The gray ones with the safety pin holding them up. Why doesn't he care that the house fell down in the corner and you can see the basement through the floor? Does he know that he parked the car in the fence last week? Is it okay for me to ask you these questions? Hey, can you teach me about carburetors? Love, Little Hans"

So frightened was Hans by the questions that his brain could ask that not only did he never send this letter, but he gave it the ritual treatment reserved for the most grave childhood promises: he would write the promise in large bold letters on a clean sheet of paper and set it ablaze in a fantastic scene crouched before the family fireplace. I WILL NEVER THINK THESE QUESTIONS AGAIN. Mostly, he never did.

8)

Hans took the bottle of vodka carefully by its neck, between thumb and fingers, and lifted it from his chest where it seemed to have sunk as if in a shallow pile of sand. He held it extended in his fingers and replaced it in the book. He set the novel back on his bedside table. It was certainly frightening to have a bottle pitch forward from out of a book. But beyond this superficial fright was a dull, deep, gray-blue sense of foreboding. Inevitability. What the bottle bode, so to speak. Bode in his bones.

Hans got up from his bed stiff and bent in the back, like a man bowed to earth with fatigue. He had to get out of this room. He would go for a walk, although he had no idea where. Dread was starting to fill him, from the feet up, as if he were a mold being filled.

He had to escape these thoughts. But how do you run from your own thoughts? He went to the door and pulled on it, but only the bottom half swung back leaving him staring at the top half. Oddly, this door which swung open from the bottom made him feel as if his torso had been sliced in half. This was not possible! When you open a door, the door is open. All the way open. Not open in the bottom, closed on the top. This door which sliced him in two seemed part of a new reality which was not disputable and which had established itself intractably in a slender, obscure corridor of his brain.

Fortunately, a vision came to him. A plump woman in white, her hair in a net, leaned against the bottom half of this door, grinning, reassuring, coffee in one hand, a cigarette in the other, flour from the morning's donuts on her arms up to her elbows. She was talking and laughing and seemed to want to say something to Hans. Maybe she wanted to tell him that there was nothing extraordinary about this kind of door. It was really a comforting, fun kind of door that you could lean your tired elbows on. (Thank God somebody somewhere, even if a ghostly phantasm, took some small interest in his well-being.) At any rate, Hans got it. He slipped the latch, opened the top, walked into the lobby and out the front door. He paused only once to check that in fact the bottom half of his body was still with him.

If part of his anxiety was about being alone, he didn't have to worry about that. Ricky was standing in front, his foot on a five-gallon plastic bucket. For a moment he looked like he was there to guard Hans's door, but it wasn't clear if he was protecting him or making sure he didn't escape. There was someone with him.

"Ah, Hans! Welcome! Did you have a pleasant nap? Cousin, I'd like you to meet someone. A very important someone in our little world. This is the Mayor. Mayor Jesse."

The Mayor extended a hand the size of a ham. It was an enormous, powerful, disgusting thing. It was the kind of hand that one made soup stock with. Moreover, Mayor Jesse had one of those bellies that give shirt designers fits. Such a belly gives up on keeping anything tucked-in. The Mayor was not a tucked-in kind of person at all. He wore a shiny brown suit. His face was jowly and he had an unfortunate nervous tick or twitch on the right side of his face. At irregular moments, the entire right side of his face would just leap into its own independent life. Unhappily, this independent life of twitches had the effect of repeatedly knocking his thick, brown glasses down the ridge of his nose. He was constantly raising his hand to readjust them, only to have the next seismic plate shift in his cheek knock them down again.

Weirdly, Ricky saluted and clicked his heels, his back hard and straight, as if to show Hans how the Mayor was to be treated. "Mr. Mayor, may I present my cousin Mr. Hans Castorp, B.S., from Downstate? He is a recent graduate of our distinguished state university system, majoring in Industrial Psychology."

Mayor Jesse greeted his new citizen with a growling, jovial outburst of twitches, drool and mostly incoherent heartiness. Showing his well-spaced, yellowing teeth, he said in a surprising falsetto, "Welcome to The Elixir. Do you come as a patient, that is to say, for the recovery?"

"Oh no, thank you, Mr. Mayor, but I'm just here for a few weeks to visit my cousin and report back to his parents on his progress."

The Mayor seemed genuinely surprised, perhaps even disappointed. "Really! By God, I'm not sure I like the sound of that! That's a wicked curve ball your cousin throws there, Ricky. I no sooner meet him than he's knockin' me off the plate! And as for Ricky and his 'progress,' my God man, that's a good one. That's a keeper. Progress, huh? Ricky here owns the God damned place. That's progress for you. Ain't that about the size of it, Ricky?"

"Nearly, Mr. Mayor."

"Nearly?"

"Nearly."

The brevity of Hans's stay made him a curiosity for the Mayor, so he continued.

"You know, Mr. Castro . . ."

"It's Castorp, Mayor Jesse," volunteered Ricky.

"Say what? CAStor? Like the oil?"

"Sort of, sir," smiled Ricky.

"Right. Good enough for me. Anyway, Hans . . . hell, I'll just go ahead and call you Hans, why don't I . . . I have never in my life met a person who couldn't use somethin' more than a month here." The genial, deranged smile never left the Mayor's face, but in his eyes there was the hint of suspicion. A sidelong doubt was cast Hans's way.

"Well, no, no thank you, I really have obligations at home that I cannot ignore."

"Work I suppose." Again, the Mayor seemed all doubt.

"Yes, in fact, it is work."

"What kinda work?"

"I have a job starting in two weeks at the Caterpillar Company."

"Oh, Cat's got another one, eh? Out there Peoria way?"

"Exactly." Hans didn't quite like the way he put it.

"Earth-movin' devices. Big fuckers. Tractors. You gonna make that sort of thing?"

"Not exactly. I won't be exactly making anything."

"You don't seem much like a workin' kinda boy to me."

The bluntness of the Mayor's last comment left Hans dumbstruck. In his heart of hearts (a place I cannot claim Hans actually knew very well), he himself didn't believe that he was "a workin' kinda boy" either. But if he acknowledged that he wasn't eager to work, would that mean that the Mayor was right and he could stay on beyond his planned two weeks? In no way was that confession in Hans's interest as he saw it at that moment.

Ricky intervened. "The Mayor is a great supporter of the important social work of Recovery. Huge machines that move earth around probably don't impress His Honor as much as they should. And he has a point if you think of the kind of spiritual movement that The Elixir effects. But perhaps he tends to overstate his case in his enthusiasm."

"Perhaps be damned," chortled the Mayor, his glasses plummeting down. "You know as well as I do that this poor earth has been moved around enough. Even a dummy like myself knows that. Push a pile of shit here, push another there. Hell, I pushed more than a few piles myself. Look around you, man! How you think those damn stinkers that we call mountains got here? Look at 'em! Good God! And now you're tellin' me that a young boy like you, with no workin' to him, the next generation so to speak, is goin' . . . well, I don't want to get into it. It's not my business. I should just leave you two to yourselves. I'm sure you got catchin' up to do, bein' cousins. So I'll leave you." And he did, staggering back toward the center of the complex, hands continuing to gesture erratically, as if he were in animated conversation with the world. He could just be heard to mutter, "Wonder why some people got eyes in their heads at all. And shit for brains. But what do I know, I'm just the Mayor around here."

Hans overheard these last words and looked earnestly at Ricky. "Do you think the Mayor was offended by my answers to his questions?"

Ricky lit a cigarette and seemed to ponder their brief interview. "Cousin, the Mayor is like life itself. He is original. But, you should know, he is never angry. Or almost never. When I have seen him angry he has been, how shall I say, not so much angry as . . . wrathful. You know, like a deity, like a god. His face becomes purplish. Divine intervention sparkles in his eyes. His glasses slip to the very tip of his nose, and you know you're in a world of trouble.

"Watch his glasses, old boy. When he's in the mood to push them back up his face, all is comical, jovial, and right with the world. But when he leaves them out there, perched on that oily precipice, and he's glowering down over them, his eyes blue like a radiant heaven, then . . . well, I don't know what to tell you. There's not really much you can do. Get out of the way if you can would be my advice."

"I'll remember that."

"Yes, bless him, the Mayor is original."

"But what in the world is wrong with his face?" braved Hans. "All those awful twitches."

"Cousin, Cousin. Careful, please. Such bravado. Believe me, you'll be fortunate if your face is not twitching before your meddlesome two weeks are up.

"Another thing to keep in mind, old boy—keep it in mind right here," he touched Hans's forehead with what appeared to be a glowing index finger, "in this flat and available part of your brain—is that the Mayor is sensitive. A very sensitive soul, indeed. He likes to think he can help everyone up here. Between the two of us, he really can't help anyone. No, God help him. Nonetheless, you should have allowed him some room to think that he could help you. It will only be that much worse if he becomes convinced that he can't. For instance, I have enough experience that I am in control of my own program"—he looked down his nose and nodded both gravely and competently at his cousin—"which is as good as saying that I can control my own fate. Even so, I will every now and then invent a crisis or a disturbing dream that I can share with him. The Mayor lives in order to interpret our dreams here. He always concludes three things: your father was an alcoholic, he emotionally neglected you, and you have the hysterical belief that someone has borrowed and then misplaced your genitals."

"My God. That's awful."

"The first two, of course, are so universally true up here that they have achieved the status of human nature. It is in the nature of fathers to be drunken and negligent. The last bit, about the genitals (or 'generals' as he calls them), is pure Mayor Jesse. He imagines that someone borrowed and misplaced his genitals. He rails on about it at Council Meetings. 'Folks ought to respect private property. They ought to take more care when they borrow something. When you borrow something, be careful where you place it, people.' Unhappily, believing that he is without the benefit of genitalia leaves the Mayor out of a lot of the fun around here. He'll apologize, 'Like to join you boys, but you know the rascal who borrowed my generals has yet to return them!' And we say, 'Oh, that's okay, we understand, Mayor Jesse. If you want to borrow ours some time, just let us know. You've been without for a while now.' And he'll say, 'Wouldn't think of depriving you boys for even a moment. You just go on and have your fun without me.' And off we go."

"You make it sound so unhinged."

Ricky shrugged. "How it is is how it is."

"You know, it's funny to think that you have a Mayor at all. What exactly does the Mayor do up here?"

"Oh, that you shouldn't underestimate. Don't misunderstand his little foibles. He does indeed have a role here. It's what we call a 'pulpy' matter."

"Pulpy?"

"You said it." Ricky was not going to pursue this pulpiness any further on his own.

"Well, what does he do that's 'pulpy'?"

Ricky was, as usual, amused by his cousin's persistence. "You're really going to get to the bottom of things, aren't you? Oh my. You're the little choo-choo that could, aren't you?"

"I'm sorry if I'm snoopy. But you have introduced me to the Mayor, and I'd like to know what counts as Mayoral duty, that's all."

In reply, Ricky took Hans by the shoulder and aimed him further east, toward the last building in the row, out beyond the Daffy's Chicken, the windowless and rusting Quonset hut. "You see that building? That's the business end of this operation. That's where the actual recovering goes on. That is also the Mayor's empire. Lots of things can happen here that the Mayor doesn't know about, but not in that building. And for a simple reason. That building is about daily recovery ritual.

"The Mayor oversees three things. The first is 'boundaries.' Who is in Recovery and who is not. That's why he was so concerned with your status. He doesn't like your ambiguity. The second is 'themes.' The Mayor is constantly urging his residents to 'distill themes.' 'Who are you that have set up home within our boundary? By what themes will we know you?' Finally, the Mayor oversees our place in history."

"Your place in history? Is he kidding?"

"We all must eventually come upon our own unique way of presenting ourselves in history. In our case, history is likely to have something to do with the Mayor's monomania for his lost genitals. There really is no other theme for him. Try to give him something else, something other than the alcoholic dad/borrowed generals matrix, like say you suggested there was something wrong with corporations running the world, and he'll get this very worried expression on his face. His eyes, mouth and certainly his glasses will collapse to the center of his face, as if they were the slopes leading up to the Pike's Peak of his nose, and he'll say, 'You're one of those fellas who is full of ideas!' By which he means, 'You should go home and take them out!'"

"He's a regular lunatic."

"Don't underestimate him, old boy. There's a level at which, in fact, the Mayor oversees our place in history in absolutely the most serious sense."

"And that all goes on right in there?" Hans looked with renewed interest at the building. "One wouldn't guess. Looks so rusty and ill-kept."

"On the inside, believe me, there's nothing left unconsidered. On the inside, all the real seriousness and life's very cement, shall I say, is provided by ritual."

"What do you mean by 'ritual'?"

Ricky took his cousin by the elbow and began walking him toward the Quonset hut. He'd explain it all to his cousin if he really wanted to know.

9

While the Reverend Boyle maintained his influence through his little "discourses," Mayor Jesse preferred the vehicle of town council meetings, at which the only order of business was the Mayor's interpretations of the "dream residue" of Elixir residents. Hence:

"Hey, oh yeah, hi Hal . . . whoa, just yeah bring that, you said it, haha, right there . . . that's fine . . . I'll see you, take care . . . I'm goin' to letcha get away with it this one time, Hal . . . honest injun . . . whoa" (facial seizure, glasses plummet and are adjusted, henceforth "*j!j*") . . . "now what we've got here, let's see, what we've got here before us, folks, is . . . some of our good Christian neighbors have pointed this out to me . . . Mr. Greenwood, has city staff had a chance to look at this? . . . good . . . and you've got maps and some diagrams for us? . . . what do you mean maps of what, Mr. Greenwood, maps and some diagrams of this dream residue before us . . . action item #1 . . . we went over this last week in Discovery . . . hey! what's that? . . . jeezus not now, Hal! . . . yes egg salad is fine for me, o' course . . . but not now . . . we got dream residue on the table . . . I got a man's brain out here before us on the table . . . okay, so Ed this is your dream-matter, right? . . . one last time, Hal, and that's my last warnin' on the matter . . . so let's take another look just to refresh ourselves . . . we got a Chevrolet . . . what's that? . . . no, it's not a Chevrolet? . . . it's an airplane? . . . sorry . . . this ain't much of a representation here . . . and you're slippin' from your seat on this airplane, right? . . . and the passenger next to you is your father . . . when did he die, Ed? . . . jeez, I remember your daddy . . . I used to spread his residue out just like I'm doin' now for you . . . man oh man . . . you see how it is with time, Hal? . . . Hal's got this theory, people, that the secret of time is that we're all already dead . . . it's a good theory, I think, 'specially for a lame-brain like Hal . . . anyway, you're slippin' from your seat and you feel like it has consequences beyond what slippin' from your seat is usually about . . . like maybe it's about fallin' thirty thousand feet from an airplane . . . maybe it's about fallin' through the center of the earth . . . so you look over to grab hold of your daddy, and you've actually got the grip on his shirt sleeve, and he turns and says to you, 'Eddie, let go, you idiot, I'm already dead' . . . at which point, well, you know . . . holdin' on to dead people don't help a poor soul like Ed here stay alive . . . so that's what we have in the minutes, people . . . so now we need a motion of some kind . . . hold it . . . what's that, Hal?" (*j!j*) ". . . returned to committee? . . . no kiddin' . . . and Ed that's okay with you? . . . you sure about this? . . . because I think I have a pretty fair idea what this dream is about . . . a negligent drunken daddy, a course that, but I think that someone has taken somethin' of Ed's . . . I'm talkin' misappropriation here, Hal . . . well . . . well . . . I'll be damned . . . maybe it was a Chevrolet? now, how do you fall thirty thousand feet from a Chevrolet? . . . jeezus, I thought city staff worked this over . . . I mean, that's a lame-ass excuse, buddy . . .

if I can't trust staff to know the difference between an airplane and a Chevrolet . . . anyway . . . okay, let's move on to the next item on the agenda . . .

"Okay, folks, for those of you who aren't familiar with how we proceed, I'll be describin' our business tonight, then . . . what's that? . . . not you, too, Hal . . . where do you get those things? . . . look at those, folks . . . Hal, hold those up there for a minute . . . God damn that's ugly . . ." (*j!j*) ". . . anyhow, what we've got here before us is a family . . . uh, and they are engaged in what I like to call a family ritual . . . it's dinner, and most of us just call it dinner, but it's also a ritual . . . if you can follow me . . . it's a ritual because it's somethin' the family does every day, good or bad, doesn't make no difference . . . now a first question before us is who is in the family . . . not now, Hal, I'm really goin' on this . . . can't you just show it to Mr. Greenwood, he'll know what to do with it . . . tell him to take an aerial photograph of it, I don't give a damn . . . yeah, fly a fuckin' airplane over it and take some pictures . . . speakin' of photographs, I'd like to thank Reverend Boyle and the Council of the Remodeled Christ for this what you call visual aid . . . and by the way" . . . (*j!j*) . . . "I'd like to know who it was wrote that letter to the Ottawa paper callin' our Christian friends the Council of the Muddled Christ . . . that's no typo . . . that's simply divisive, folks . . . that separates neighbor from neighbor, don't it? . . . I mean it tends toward that, if you see my point . . . now you see this picture has mom and the oldest boy, a blondie, and two younger sisters at the table . . . everybody's all smiles . . . look at those nice kids . . ." (*j!j*) ". . . let's see what they're eatin' . . . look's like what we used to call goulash . . . hamburger and macaroni and canned tomatoes . . .

and then that would be Eyetalian green beans with bacon, and that's canned cream corn and mostly rawish bacon . . . and what would you call that there, Mr. Greenwood, a legal opinion if you please . . . very good, sir, a tub of margarine if you please, a tub of kinda grayish margarine it is, then . . . okay, folks, what's missin' here? . . . yes granny's missin', Hal, we know that, but granny's a pain in the butt and outside the family boundary at this point, don't you see? . . . don't you remember where they put her? . . . anything else missin'? . . . yes by God that's right Daddy's missin' . . . now how did this come about? . . . well, one day in the middle of well-defined ritual space—and that's what makes this possible at all, folks—Dad said he wasn't goin' to join the family for dinner just yet because he was watchin' somethin' on TV . . . the God damned Blue-Gray game was on! . . . who cares about the Blue-Gray game? . . . Hal, you know someone who cares about the fuckin' Blue-Gray game? . . . no, sir, you do not . . . the miracle of that football game is that someone watches it at all because all the players are from Tuscaloosa Tech or some damned infernal place and it's all supposed to bring back warm fuzzies about the Civil War but it's been politically incorrect for forty years to mention the fact that in this football game they're re-fightin' that war . . . especially just in case the Gray happened to win and someone wanted to be happy about it . . . and it's almost all NEGROES, Hal, NEGROES! if you can believe that . . . the civil war bein' re-fought by NEGROES from Tuscaloosa Tech . . . now, who thought that up, Hal, and what's it mean? . . . it some kind of symbol, Hal? . . . so anyway that's all part of Dad's genius here, he's watchin' this political nightmare roll out as national pastime and assertin' that it's more important than sittin' down to dinner in ritual time and space with his family . . . and that ain't all, Hal, get this, folks, if you follow me, HE EXPECTS THEM TO SIT THERE AND WAIT DON'T TOUCH A DAMNED THING UNTIL HE'S DONE . . . and for this peccadillo some folks say dad is the asshole of the family body . . . later (I'm talkin' decades here) they call out to see what quarter it is, how much time is left . . . yeah, who's winnin', Dad? . . . because there's some greasy horror formed on the green beans . . . Dad? . . . hell, he's not even home . . . he's out . . . he's down to the Brutal Inn and Out havin' a hot toddy . . . how much time we got left, Hal? . . . time to go? . . . okay, Mr. Clerk, can you read me what you got there, for the minutes?"

"Mr. Mayor, I have, 'Family regulatory behaviors now actually play a major role in maintaining chronic alcoholic behavior.' "

"Is that what I said? . . . okay, if I said that then I said that . . . you do good work, Mr. Clerk . . . that's it folks . . . thank you all most kindly . . . I have every confidence . . ."

10)

Alone again in his room that evening, Hans thought about the Mayor and what Ricky had told him of his leadership style at meetings. The Mayor was quite a character and yet, Hans felt, he was very familiar in some odd way. He was fat in a way Hans found frightening. And he was as pale as he was fat. Mayor Jesse seemed to have a way of being fat that was an explicit confession, an acknowledgement, of what fat is. He made Hans think of the stuff that formed at the top of cans of chicken soup. And you could say in a moment exactly what his diet had been for the last two decades. Donuts, coffee, beef, pork and cheap beer. Lots of that. Hans had to wonder how people like this made it through a day on such a regimen, and yet they seemed to live long lives. If life were some sort of endurance race, Hans was not confident he could win out over such a one as the Mayor, in spite of the presence of a few fruits and vegetables in his own diet.

And then—what had Ricky told him?—the Mayor fancied himself to be some sort of psychoanalyst! He wanted to hear everyone's dreams! That took the cake. What in the world did he do with these dreams? Ricky said that, for example, he had related to the Mayor a recent dream in which he had "accidentally" knocked a massive, redwood deck chair from a second-story window and it had just narrowly missed his piano teacher or basketball coach or chemistry teacher, someone like that, who sat on the patio below.

Ricky said that the Mayor had become quite animated in his eagerness to "interpret" the dream. "By God, man, by God. Don't you see? You're trying to say something. Something important. This dream, this dream is an expression of your hidden rage with your father for his years of drunkenness and emotional neglect. Ain't all chemistry teachers our fathers? The idea that it could have been your sweet old piano teacher is just a mean misdirection. The temptation to think that it could have been your piano teacher is like following a buzzing barnyard fly. Fat one. And I suspect he may have taken something from you, something very important, when you were young and couldn't defend yourself. Don't deny it! Now, I want you to think. Think, man! What did he take from you? Say it! Starts with a big *G*. And now you want, subconscious-like, to hurt him! What do you think of that? So you drop the old patio furniture on him from the second floor! Sure you do! And they say dreams are all in your head! By God, man!"

Hans wondered if the Mayor would want to hear the dream he had had on his first night there:

Ricky was driving a large tractor. It was a monster tractor. Its wheels loomed blackly high over Hans's head. Ricky had huge muscles like a pumped-up war doll, some sort of steroid-inflated G. I. Joe. His T-shirt was torn at the sleeves from the strain. Ricky was laughing and looking back as he drove. Behind him he pulled a harvest bin used for collecting husked corn. Just over the edge of the bin—Hans's dream perspective seemed to be floating above them now, which added a certain giddiness to the scene, as if he were a large, chubby balloon hovering over Macy's Thanksgiving Day Parade—Hans could see the heads of children, mostly boys, lifting up and calling out. They were complaining. "Those in charge should behave with more reason!" said one. "When teeth bite, they sink in a little," said another. "When I am a girl of sixteen, I will sit one day in the living room of my parents' home and sew at a round table," said the largest of the boys. It all seemed strange because while they acted desperate, their words were controlled. Plainly, though, they wanted out of the bin, but the sides were simply too steep. They ran up and slid back down, their little arms outstretched, like mice fallen in a bucket. Ricky seemed to find their efforts and their words funny.

Boy, thought Hans, what would the Mayor make of this? He groaned to imagine it. "Folks, we hear a lot here in Discovery. But there are some things I won't ask you to endure. Just go on home, now. But Mr. Hans, buddy, I want to talk with you alone. No, Darlene, you don't have to feel obliged to console the newcomer. He's a big boy and he can take a little responsibility for his dreams, bizarre and offensive though they may be."

Well, it was light out now anyway. He might as well get up. He'd better just get up and have some coffee.

Ah! Coffee! Hans Castorp adored coffee. So addicted to this pleasure was he, such a precocious little connoisseur was he, that he'd actually brought his own handsomely engineered German coffee-maker, a grinder and a supply of perfectly dark-roasted beans grown on a tiny volcanic island off the coast of Africa. Coffee was his morning ritual, his afternoon ritual and his evening ritual. In fact, one might say it was the only thing in God's bright world that Hans knew of a cultivated human pleasure. He would make coffee in the clear light of reason. In the morning freshness.

Hans shuddered to think what Mr. Donut coffee might have been like. Or what they served at the Daffy's. Duck coffee, ugh! Or what boiled in the aluminum cisterns at the Quonset hut!

He smiled and opened a Ziploc bag full of his favorite beans. He thought again vaguely about the little island where they had come from. How nice it must be there. He saw the native boys lithe as frogs leaping from cliffs into a bright sea. On the shore people clad all in white linen smiled and looked on, a fine porcelain cup of coffee in their hands. He cupped in his hand a golden coffee filter as if it were an infant cranium, relic of an obscure but very personal saint. He measured the beans into the grinder. He pressed the switch, anticipating the satisfying racket, the familiar whirring of the blades pulverizing the beans, a self-possessed if not smug expression on his face. But there was no sound, at least no sound from the grinder. He checked the plug in its socket. It was firm. He plunged again. He did hear something this time. He was having one of those forceful co-incidental experiences that immediately call all of one's assumptions about cause and effect into question. Like turning the ignition on the car and hearing the neighbor's lawn mower. Like pressing the trigger on a power tool at just the moment that a siren goes off. When Hans pushed the button on his coffee grinder, he heard not the grinder but a different, though not distant, noise. He took his finger off the button, but this time the noise continued. He was still confused, but at least now he was sure that the sound wasn't coming from his coffee grinder. Where was it coming from? It seemed to be coming from beneath his feet. He bent to the floor and listened. There was a loud, high-pitched buzzing, one might call it a vicious buzzing, as if from a mosquito the size of a dental drill. Then he thought he heard a mournful moaning made by someone who authentically hated anything chaste. All this seemed to make its way up through the floor and up his bare feet and legs. Then, just as suddenly as it had begun, it stopped, as if it were really just a slightly off-kilter furnace fan that had finished its cycle.

But now vaguely, in its aftermath, didn't he hear a ghost choir of lost boys quietly singing, "I'll have a blue Christmas without you . . ."?

Hans decided that he could have his coffee later. He had to escape these sounds now, before he began to imagine what they in fact were. So he dressed quickly and went out through the Mr. Donut lobby.

The brisk morning was, for Hans, simply optimism. The sky seemed a ceramic blue, as if the place were contained by an enormous enameled bowl. Directly across the road, a field of corn muttered dryly, its leaves echoing under the pottery sky like small sticks clicking together. The air itself smelled unnaturally pure. The stinking wind of boiling tennis balls and plastic thongs was gone. Now the air seemed sterile, as if it were being filtered through gauze soaked in alcohol. Hans even felt a kind of astringent stinging in his nose. He looked through this limpid if not quite living air down the row of incongruous buildings. In this light, the weird edifices looked harmless. Hans was glad to see this. Perhaps, he thought, my impressions yesterday were all just fatigue. Yes. New places are always intimidating when you are tired. He decided that he just needed to get used to the place.

At that moment Hans noticed that Ricky was again waiting for him, eternal warden, sitting not five steps away on the plastic bucket.

He leaned forward, elbows on knees, breaking dry chunks of dark soil with his hands. He'd already accumulated a little hill, not unlike the slag heaps that loomed over and behind them. Once again, Hans had the unnerving feeling that his cousin was some sort of bored sentry stationed at his door.

"Morning, Cousin."

"Good morning, Ricky. What are you doing?"

"Just waiting for you. Aren't we going to have breakfast together?"

Hans took a deep breath. The idea of eating with his cousin made him tense. "Breakfast. Yes, I'd like that." To the contrary, Hans felt as if he were being pulled back into a particularly unpleasant dream.

Ricky got up, smiled rakishly, gestured broadly with his arms, as if to say, "This way, my lord," and the two began strolling back toward the dark Daffy's.

"So. Did you sleep well? Bed comfy?"

"Yes. Thanks."

"No complaints about the accommodations?"

"No, but . . . ," and here Hans paused, looked uneasily at his cousin, unsure what consequences might follow from describing his coffee grinder experience.

"What, Cousin?" Ricky had stopped and taken Hans, tenderly enough, by his elbow. But something in his eye said, in this place, old boy, you will confess every thought. "A bad dream?"

"Dream? Heavens no, no dreams," Hans lied. This was his first shrewd gesture, his first tacit acknowledgment that some things might be best left unsaid here at The Elixir. This shrewd gesture was all the more impressive due to the fact that he was in truth terrified to imagine that somehow Ricky knew he had dreamed, and he wanted to scream, "You are in my head! Admit it! Somehow you are in my head!"

"You know, old boy, if by some chance you had dreamed, it would be a marvelous opportunity to share it with the Mayor. As I've told you, he likes to help with dreams. He'd be very pleased to discover that you, too, have dreams and that he might help you with them."

"No, no dreams, I swear. But I did hear something strange this morning."

"Please, tell me about it."

At first it had seemed such a relief not to have to confess to his dream that merely telling about the weird sounds coming from beneath his floor seemed merciful. But now that he was confronted with having to acknowledge the sounds, he didn't like that option much either. Ricky, however, seemed almost caring, which gave Hans courage. In fact, he supposed that he had no concrete reason to think that Ricky wasn't caring. There had been some strange, or awkward, maybe even difficult, moments on his first day, but Ricky was probably just trying to help Hans get his bearings in a new environment. Ricky simply had an exceptionally frank nature. That was all. And if Hans was sensitive to Ricky's manner, well, that could be, after all, as much Hans's problem as Ricky's. For Hans had been told by others that he "hated to look facts in the face."

Hans began, still a little timidly. "Well, when I pressed the button on my coffee grinder this morning, I heard not the grinding of beans, because the grinder didn't seem to work at all; I heard a high pitched buzzing, as if from an enormous mosquito, and then a sort of struggling, panting, and moaning sound followed by the faint strains of a

Christmas song and all seeming to come up through the floor of my room. Is there someone below me? Below the donut store?"

Ricky considered what his cousin told him quietly and seriously. It was as if he were being told something that he knew to be a lie and, further, knew that the person lying to him couldn't know that he knew. He had that sort of masterful "you really shouldn't mess with me" air. "Hmmm," he said at last. Then, looking his cousin dead in the eye, "Do you mean to tell me that you brought your own coffee and a coffee grinder here? Carried it in your bag all the way from Downstate?"

Hans answered fearfully, "Yes, I did. Is there something wrong with that?" There was nothing aggressive in Hans's question. It was anxious, it was abject, it was frightened. It was as if he really expected to be told what he had done wrong. What he had done badly and stupidly. He felt that every time he opened his mouth he revealed something about himself, like paring away his own flesh.

"Well, old boy," Ricky was grinning in a malevolent, toothy way, "I'd say that if your coffee grinder is not grinding coffee and is making moaning sounds, there's something bloody well wrong with it. If I were you, I'd throw it to hell away in a garbage can."

11

The Reverend Phenues Boyle Further Discourses upon Family Ritual

Now, there are many things that are in fact family rituals which are not usually recognized as such. Dad's power over the TV is but one of these ritual formations. Let me put it to you this way: the family "geometry," if you will (i.e., the relation of oracular TV to priestly father [he who knows what "channels" carry the family fate] to awestruck and reverent children to serviceable mother who carries the sacred bowls to and from the kitchen, cupped in her hands, brimming with fudge and popcorn), Is As It Is. It is ordained. It is not to be given over to analysis. It is Holy. When tampered with, it becomes blasphemous, or an abomination.

And the gestures by which this ruin is wrought—the television remote in the sticky, irresponsible fingers of a daughter, as I have described for you *en exemplum*—can seem so innocent to us. Why not let little Suzy sit in Daddy's chair and press the buttons for an evening? What harm can come of it? Well, What Harm Comes To Them If The Floor Of Their Home Falls Away As If They Were Criminals Being Hanged, And Sofa, Lights And Everyone Else

Plummeting Through a Trap Door Into A Muddy Sea Of Corpses Upon Which Their Suburban Glory Is Built And From Which They Are Protected Only By The Rigorous Maintenance Of Family Ritual In Family Ritual Space?!

Let me provide you with another example of the "harmless" activities that have come to threaten family health. This is called by some "Women's Night Out" or "Girls' Night." Oh, this is a favorite of the so-called "emancipated." The ladies involved think this one is quite funny. "Liberated," as they put it, flatulently. For they imagine that in claiming the "night" they usurp a male perquisite. And you know what? In claiming the night they usurp a male perquisite! That is exactly the damnable hell of it!

Now, one of the things that girls will do on their "night" is get together to play cards. On one night with one family that I am aware of, four ladies had gathered in the home of wife Suzy, let us call her, to play canasta with Wanda, Dolores and Vivian (Vi). (And was there not arrogance and rebellion in the simple fact that they *knew* how to play this card game canasta?) Husband Tom, let us call him, tried to play the "enlightened" male and volunteered to serve the ladies. Well, the game as such was not as interesting to these ladies as the great quantities of execrable white zinfandel they imbibed and at a certain hour, oh lord, the tales their lubricated tongues did tell.

On this one celebrated evening, the girls were swapping stories about their most recent visits to a nearby "stud" show. There they could find the thrusting Malatestas, swarthy Italian fellows who bared all, masquerading as murderous, dancing *condotiers*. In fact, they were moonlighting members of World Wrestling Entertainment. Sigismundo, Ardent Arnaut, and Cavalcanti (Terminator, Mr. Death, and Man Mountain in other venues) writhed lewdly to Whitney Houston or Prince or, their trademark, Palestrina set to a disco beat. At the end of the performance, five dollar bills stuffed in their already over-stuffed crotches, they'd flex enormously, their tongues flicking at the moon, snake-mad and bestial.

Well, their talk, of course, led them to wonder if perhaps, after another round of pinkish zin, they wouldn't be ready to head on out there. Catch bodacious Sigismundo and his nefarious Dagger Boys in their last show. And they might have gone then if Tom hadn't overheard their heated chitchat. For their saucy talk was a ragout, thickening, clotting. A sly look in his eyes, he excused himself and when he returned he was wearing only tennis shoes, an apron ("The Crystal Cruet: Gifts and Gourmet Stuff"), and a wicked smile.

"I don't think you girls need to go out. If you need a show, I can put on a show for you," he said, arms akimbo. And they all looked at him, surprised but a little delighted at the sleazy nastiness of it. It's amazing that bad zinfandel can make a bag of bones look good. When Tom made his first pass around the table, all the girls could see his baby-white butt encircled by soft black hair like a rear-end tonsure. Only Wanda laughed a bit, perhaps out of a guilty tension, perhaps because in fact Dad was in his late thirties and had not even a passing acquaintance with a Nautilus machine and so looked passing-silly with his skinny white shanks, vodka belly and sallow, sagging jowls. No Ardent Arnaut this guy.

But for the rest of them, they were not shy about caressing Dad's pastry butt as he came by, bowl of chips in hand. Mom, of course, knowing Dad's mostly soggy gifts all too well, only watched and gave her approval to her friends with little winks.

By the end of a very frenzied half-hour, Dad was bent over the card table with one of Vi's shapeless and wrinkled breasts in his mouth, Wanda was crouched under the table about to peek beneath Dad's apron, and Dolores had unearthed a monstrosity from the depths of her handbag, had strapped it to her waist, enhanced it with slick tahini and plunged it in Dad's *cavus anterior.* And, my God, the man claimed to like it! Yes, he seemed even to meow with his approval and thrust his bony haunches a little higher for her convenience.

And then Wanda did in fact seek the gifts beneath his Crystal Cruet apron but promptly re-emerged, a look of surprise and disappointment on her face.

She asked Mom, "Honey, is this his penis?"

"Of course," she replied, a little embarrassed, ashamed perhaps of his scanty treasure, or of girl-legends-past which were now being shown as inflated. "What else would be there?"

"Are you sure?"

"Well, I think so. That's where he is used to keeping his penis."

"But is this his erection?"

And then Dad got in on the debate, allowing Vi's breast to flop down from his mouth. "What are you talking about, for God's sake? Yes, that's my penis! What in the world are you thinking about? I am erect."

And old Wanda ducked back down in order to check her findings but quickly bobbed back up saying, "Well, I don't want to be an alarmist, but when was the last time anyone performed an inventory down here?"

Now, as you can see, this is a horror, this is a human monstrosity working its way out, but it would not work its way out because another horror was in development because life outside of routine family ritual is horror piled on horror.

From off to the side, a side obscured in shadows, in a darkened living room recess, looking in on these bewildering adult pranks, came a tiny voice, "Mommy, what are you and Daddy doing?"

"Oh, my God, Tom, you forgot to put the children to bed!"

And there, certainly, sat the three betrayed modern children, little Klerk and his two younger sisters, Magma and Compulsa, all tiny, teary eyes and trauma. Dolores removed the mean apparatus from Dad's *cavus* with a queasy plopping noise, and looked to Suzy for direction.

"Girls, I think that's it for tonight," said sadder-but-wiser Suzy.

And they began indeed sadly to pull themselves together for their despairing rides home to their own flaccid husbands when, *mirabile dictu*, the children jumped from their seats and in jumping were transformed into bats, tiny black bats, which flew and swooped about the room, screaming in their awful pain and the ladies on their night out were running away (as best they could in a prefab diningroom that was only 12' x 12') screaming like the pig into which Jesus had thrown a demon. "Ahhh, the brats are going to make a nest in my hair!" shrieked Wanda.

And so when you are travelling down Illinois's country roads, and you see one of our state-of-the-art hog confinement facilities, and you see the containment lagoons, spreading like the last shitten wetland, and you see the edifice, a high-rise pig tenement housing fifty-thousand, and you hear their multitudinous screams, ask not, penitents, "Why do you scream so? And why do you behave like this?"

It is because the pigs are foul, the pigs are a foul people, and Jesus needs more pigs, but these tiny children were not pigs, they were bats, don't forget, and were flying madly about the heads of these ladies on their sacred "night out," squealing, looking for nesting spots in the big-hair these ladies sported, where they could burrow down, clamp their lancet claws in scalp and lay a new brood of bat eggs.

And where, you might well ask, was Daddy Tom during this melee? Take a peek beneath the cloth that covers their canasta table. Yes, that's him, knees clutched to his chest, a tiny testicle shrunken by environmental hormone mimickers squirting out between his thighs, a rattled expression in his eyes, all shit and fear, while overhead, the world flies apart, flies into its separate pieces, scatters in vast inter-galactic winds.

Thus, friends, the inner sanctum of domestic life in the aftermath of the demise of fatherly ritual.

12

As Hans and his cousin approached the Daffy's and the promise of breakfast, Hans couldn't help noticing that The Elixir, quite unlike the day before, was now teeming and busy. It was like a scene from his old college cafeteria, or the Downstate shopping mall on a busy weekend. People were everywhere. For some reason, the sight of all these people helped Hans to relax. Perhaps it was simply a matter of seeing that he was not alone. Or, if he was alone, that these "others" were so many in number that they couldn't all be dangerous. There had to be some kind folk here. Surely, some of them would help him if he needed help.

Ricky seemed to say good morning to everyone they passed, and they all not only recognized him but knew him quite well. Mothers and their children swarmed by and called out, "Good morning, Mr. Ricky. It's pleasant this morning, isn't it? Children, say good morning to Mr. Ricky."

"Good morning, Mr. Ricky!"

All of which Hans thought was very cute. "Mr. Ricky, is it?" he joked to his cousin.

"What's funny about that, old boy?"

"Well, they call you Mr. Ricky as if you were bearded authority itself."

Ricky looked his cousin in the eye, a blunt gesture that Hans was growing wary of.

"In a way, I am. I am 'bearded authority' here. You'll see. It's not like back home. I'm no bad seed here. Not my mother's rotten apple or a black sheep either. Perhaps it amuses you to see someone treated with real respect, but I have *earned*—I emphasize that strange word for you—a very particular respect here."

Just then a woman—distinctly housewife-ish, in a worn cloth coat, frumpy to her soul, the archetypal Midwestern Wal-Mart lost-shopping-soul—came by with two unhealthy looking children of uncertain but soiled gender in tow. Just as the others had done, she said, "Good morning, Mr. Ricky," but she said it with an unmistakable leer, a not-so-veiled suggestion that shocked Hans.

"Did you see that woman look at you, Ricky? I swear she was grinning at you shamefully. In broad daylight. It's a bit thick. A fat, disheveled thing like that. What can she be thinking?"

Ricky smiled enigmatically. "I told you, Cousin. I am admired here." Then he looked at Hans sternly, as if he were his tutor. "And what the hell do you know about what is or isn't desirable in a woman?"

Hans blushed, sorry he'd ventured into this terrain. "Not a lot, I grant you. But I doubt that a fat thing like that would stand much of a chance with a person like you, even if you aren't entirely well."

"Hans, have you ever had sex while watching TV?"

"No."

"Then shut up."

Hans had no idea what his cousin was implying, but he was happy to shut up since this conversation terrified him. Still, he wasn't a lot happier with embarrassed silence. So he asked, "Where were all of these people yesterday? I swear I thought the place was a ghost town, but now it looks like most of Central Illinois is here." The commotion really was loud.

"You simply haven't seen all of our facilities yet, old boy. These six buildings are just what we call downtown. This complex is vast."

"Really? Vast where?" Hans asked both skeptically and logically.

Ricky dodged the question. "This is, after all, the central state facility for recovery. When souls go into receivership, this is where they're sent. When you arrived yesterday, most of our residents were at the Late Cure which has been known to go on till three o'clock in the morning."

"Three o'clock in the morning!"

"Oh, it's intense."

"Well, how can they look so fresh, then, so early in the day?"

"They don't all stay up so late. The children, for example, usually pass out much earlier. And many of the mothers are not up to the rigors of Cure. You will notice that there are not so many men here this morning. The social obligation or, one might say, community burden for recuperation is square on the backs of the men. They often don't have their first meal until ten or eleven."

"But, Ricky, you still haven't answered my question. Where are all of these people? Where do they stay?"

"We've annexed some of the smaller local towns. Carbon Hill, for example, is entirely ours. Still lots of paperwork to be done, of course. It will take time for people to get used to the idea that whole towns can be recovery institutions, even while it's obvious that the whole town is in need of it. But until then . . ."

"Until then?"

"A large percentage of our residents are underground."

"Underground? Are you joking?"

Suddenly, like a voice inserted in dream, someone asked, "Breakfast, sir?"

Hans had been so engrossed in this conversation that he hadn't noticed that he had not only arrived at the cafeteria but that he had gone down the food line with an empty tray. Behind the counter, barely visible through the steam coming up from around a vat of oatmeal, was little Teddy. Seeing Teddy again presented Hans with a whole new set of anxieties, so that he forgot about what it might mean for all of these people to be living "underground," perhaps even right under his feet. He was more concerned, for the moment, with whether or not Teddy was going to pick up where they had left off the day before. Fortunately, Teddy was "on task."

"Good morning, Teddy. How are you?"

"Fine, sir. Breakfast, sir?"

Hans looked with suspicion at the offerings. No condiment packets this time. Rather, the pans were full of oatmeal with raisins, French toast, bacon, and scrambled eggs. Lovely. Hans particularly enjoyed the rich, pastiness of powdered scrambled eggs, a principal pleasure of his dorm days. Hans also noticed, however, in a moment that can only be described as "unlovely," that Teddy seemed still to be wearing yesterday's T-shirt. He couldn't help but remember what he would see on it if Teddy were to turn around. The thought set limits on his appetite.

"I'll have some oatmeal, Teddy, and a serving of the eggs."

"Right-o, sir. Oatmeal and eggs coming up."

Hans took his food and moved down the line toward the coffee, for which he practically drooled.

But Teddy wasn't quite done. "Oh, and sir, I was thinking about what we were discussing yesterday."

Hans paled. A woman standing behind him looked on with considerable curiosity. "Yes, Teddy?"

"I'd like to have the opportunity some time, sir, to point out to you a few of the inconsistencies pertaining to your own stated position vis-à-vis certain so-called social inequalities."

The woman caught Hans's eye and nodded in Teddy's direction, as if to say, "He is the little scholar, isn't he?"

"For instance, I don't believe, in all due respect, sir, that you have sufficiently thought through the social implications of the fact that our laws do not prevent us from killing animals whether for food or sport."

Hans had no idea what Teddy was referring to, but he feared that the boy's capacity for logical consequence had raced on several steps beyond his own limited capability. Hans felt a strange but increasingly familiar sinking. The woman simply smiled as if charmed by the urchin's precocity.

"So," Teddy continued, gesturing with a large metal spoon from which oatmeal trickled thickly into a counter top quagmire, "the right to life of animals is nonexistent. This is especially so during times of war, general crisis, or when people simply aren't at home with their feelings. I'd like to know if you agree, sir, as it could be a significant factor in our subsequent discussions. I think it could have a bearing on just what humans deserve. For instance, are humans not animals? Do humans have rights beyond what we give to other animals?"

There was something vaguely accusatory in what he said. It was as if Teddy knew that, for reasons that even Hans couldn't imagine, that Hans couldn't agree with him, or couldn't agree with him enough to prevent the next implacable step in his dangerous logic.

The woman now touched Hans's hand very gently and said, "He's a little philosopher, isn't he?"

Hans rubbed the spot where she'd touched him as if it were burned.

"I don't know," he said lamely, staring over the counter at Teddy's slightly dizzying image, "I really don't know."

Little Teddy returned his stare confidently.

"He's one of those liberals," said Teddy.

"I see," said the woman.

"Be careful with him. You know how they can twist your thoughts around."

"I'll be very careful."

"Talk to you later, sir."

"Goodbye, Teddy."

Hans lifted his tray and left the line, looking for his cousin. But Ricky had already found a table at which, unhappily, there were no more chairs. Ricky caught Hans's eye and shrugged, as if to say, "So what of it? Better luck next time. You're on your own."

For her part, the woman seemed to think this made Hans her breakfast companion.

"There are two seats over there. Shall we take them?"

At that moment, our young Hans felt simply like the emotionally neglected child of divorced parents, shuttlecocking between them on bruising volleys, neither really very much interested in having him around. A little flash of childish anger flared in him, as if he would pitch a fit, throw a tantrum, or at least display some self-preserving, if also infantile, obstinacy. (You see, his emotional repertoire was larger than simply being cowed, fragile and subservient.) But just as he was pulling together the elements of his face so that when they burst back out they'd go a really long way, in his fury, this woman smiled sweetly, nodded, gestured with her head, her eyes just a little imploring, as if to say, "Look, I'm not so bad. You'll like me. You won't regret this." And casting a last confused look down on the bloated raisins that littered his oatmeal, he pushed forward.

So, for the first time, Hans was adrift from his only human mooring at The Elixir. It has to be said, though, that as moorings go Ricky was hardly the most sturdy. He was more like the concrete piling against which a little boat could really get slammed. His new companion, on the other hand, seemed from the first all smiles and consideration. She was perhaps forty-five-years-old and a little chunky. She wore her hair pinned back very properly. Hans's first thought about her was, "My God, she looks like the librarians at Downstate. Will I be stuck with a librarian up here?" His second thought, however, reversed this first 180 degrees. It was founded on the neckline of her blouse. She wore a nice, white modest blouse which if it didn't exactly plunge it could easily be said to dip down toward the first hint of a handsome, one might say "motherly," cleavage which flashed so limpid white that it must never have seen the sun in all of its forty-five years. This cleavage seemed to say to Hans,

"Ask if you can see me!" And this idea caused in Hans such a stirring as only a twenty-two-year-old can know, the sort of stirring that just wants to leap out, and so he was about to say, "Can I see your . . ." what? cleavage? breasts? lungs? Hans had no idea what would really satisfy his need to see, but instead he said, in a spasm of stupidity of the sort for which one blushes for life, "Are you a librarian?"

Fortunately, this woman took his question well, although she was also amazed by it. "No," she replied, laughing, "I'm not a librarian at all. I was a CPA until several years ago when I became ill and came here."

Hans cringed. "I'm sorry. That was a rude question. And we've just met. I mean, we haven't even met yet. I'm Hans Castorp. I graduated from Downstate University last week, and I'm here visiting my cousin Ricky."

"Yes, I've seen you with the august Ricky. My name is Cecile. And I'm . . . here too."

"I can see you are," replied Hans still in a small panic. He had no idea what to say next. Mostly he was afraid that his brain would fixate again on meeting Cecile's breasts, so in a sort of lunacy he began looking at all the things on the table—jam, honey, butter, fruit, carafes of coffee—and grinning.

"Is breakfast always a funny meal for you?" asked Cecile, amazed by his behavior and nearly as amused by it as Hans seemed to be by the pot of honey, although with more reason.

"No," replied Hans, trying now to gain some sort of control over the expressions that stampeded across his face. "No. I don't always find breakfast funny."

Now his companion sat, regarding him carefully and smiling at his awkwardness, enjoying the mad energy he was trying to control.

Just when Hans thought he might gain some control over himself, there was a loud and very male explosion of laughter behind him. It was Ricky's table. Ricky was talking rapidly and smiling, as if he were sharing some very funny stories. Several of his companions looked over conspicuously at Hans.

"Well, would you like some honey?"

"What?"

Cecile was handing the pot of honey to Hans.

"Do you put honey on your oatmeal, or do you prefer to merely grin at your breakfast."

"Yes, I'd like some, thanks." He took the pot from her. It was sticky with honey. Cecile put her fingers to her mouth while holding Hans's stare. Her fingers must have had honey on them too. Hans's mouth hung open.

His own earlier words to Ricky returned: "a bit thick."

"The honey is a bit thick," he said.

"Honey is usually thick," she smiled, eating her food. Once again she was the celibate librarian. Or CPA. Or whatever she was.

"By the way, Cecile is not my real name."

"It's not?"

"No. It's my *nomme du guerre*. My *nomme du jour*. We all go by different names here. It's part of our culture of anonymity. It's a very important part of feeling safe enough to reveal things, emotions, that are either painful or not easily acceptable under ordinary circumstances."

"You mean reveal things at the Mayor's City Council Meetings?"

"Oh, so you've met the Mayor already. Yes, there and elsewhere."

"But what about my cousin. His name is really Ricky."

"Ah, your cousin," said Cecile, buttering a piece of toast. "Ricky is Ricky. You're right about that. But he *is* different." She gave Hans a very meaningful look that Hans was unable even to begin to understand. "You'll see. He's among us but not of us. He lives at his own level. He's above identity and anonymity. He says what he wants and everyone else scrambles to adjust. He's really . . . how do I want to say this . . . an original. Your cousin is a force of nature." She looked at Hans. "Do you know what I mean?"

"I think so. Ricky and the Mayor are powerful here."

"No, no. The Mayor has authority. It's different. His authority—not to be taken lightly—also makes him ludicrous. But there's nothing ludicrous about your cousin. The only other that approaches him is the Reverend Boyle."

"I haven't met him yet."

"Of course you haven't. You've been with Ricky. You won't often meet the Reverend if you're with Ricky. When those two are together, watch out." She cast her eyes up across the ceiling as if tracking a firework.

"They don't get along?"

"Oh, they get along, all right. It's what happens to anyone around them that you need to worry about."

"Really!"

"I spent just one evening with those two!" She laughed and looked off into some glad and painful space. She returned her look right between Hans's eyes and said, "Ouch!" Then she laughed loudly, pushing herself back in her chair.

"Ouch?"

"Ouch!" She continued laughing. "It was great fun, but never again, not if I can help it. But don't you worry about it. You'll meet the Reverend at the right moment."

Poor Hans. The Elixir was overwhelming for him in even its most rudimentary terms. And now he had to acknowledge what he had no courage to acknowledge, this Cecile, his first adult acquaintance here, was a vast intellectual drama in herself. He began to feel how intensely he was the Downstate "hick."

Cecile continued. "Oh, and the children, of course."

"What about them?"

"Well, they use their own names, too. But, you know, it's so hard to be sure what to do with children. Do they count as human? Or not? No one here has ever been very clear about it, not even the mothers. Perhaps Teddy could enlighten us. But, do you see my point?"

Hans hesitated. "I think I do. You mean because children are not yet mature, and so are not like adults? Is that what you mean?"

"Not really. For myself, I like to think of them as puppets."

"Puppets?"

Hans stared dumbly at Cecile who laughed a full healthy, happy, harmless sort of middle-aged laugh. "Exactly," she said.

"What is your real name, then, if it's not Cecile?" said Hans, eager to change the subject.

"Mr. Castorp!" she replied, coquettishly. "That's a very personal question! We've only just met! What would people think!"

"I'm sorry."

"Okay," she agreed, leaning towards Hans over the table, her chin nearly in her breakfast, her eyes bright with the naughtiness of the moment, "I'll tell you. But this is just between you and me. My name is Frau X."

"Frau X?"

"Yes."

"That's your real name?"

"Yes. It's German."

"I see."

"Well, you don't seem very pleased." Cecile sat back in her chair now, as if she had given in to Hans's truest desire—to see her cleavage fully exposed—only to find him coolish about them, maybe even disappointed.

"I don't know what to say."

"Never mind," her characteristic playful smile returned to her face. "Why don't you tell me your real name, Herr Castorp?"

"But that is my real name. Hans Castorp."

"Oh, come on! Are there a lot of little German boys named Hans at Downstate? Are you downstate from Berlin?"

"No. It really is my name though."

She slapped her hand down on the table. "Come on! I can see that you don't play fair at all." She eyed him. "I like that in a man."

"What do you want me to do? Make something up?"

Now she was the disappointed one. "Of course I want you to make something up. Isn't that what you just did? It's exciting. Especially when you make up a good one. What if you told me that your real name was Lorenzaccio! But I don't want you to *tell* me that you're going to make it up before making it up. That's boring. If only I could think that you were lying about that, too!" She had a pained expression. "You'll just have to stop being so earnest."

Cecile looked if not through Hans then into him far enough to see the dense little black marble that was his consciousness. But we shouldn't give up hope. After all, the brilliant cosmos once flashed from such a dense, black dot.

Cecile changed the subject. "So, tell me about Industrial Psychology. You must know a lot about it." She smiled a synthetic smile, one part curiosity, one part detached amusement, and one part certainty that, if she liked, Hans was nothing more than a morsel.

Hans was confused. "How did you know that I studied IP?"

"Why, you said so, I believe."

"I don't think so."

"Well, then I must have heard it somewhere."

Hans, of course, was not so sure he liked the idea that these residents could "hear" things about him, but he tried to look beyond that and answer her question. "People really don't understand what IP is about. They think it has to do with helping people with their problems. Counseling them. So-called talk therapy hasn't been a part of any kind of psychology, let alone Industrial Psychology, since the early years of the century. You probably recall the Universal De-certification Rider, part of the Fraudulent Therapies Omnibus Legislation. Congress attached it as a rider to the National Parks Re-authorization. It was a famous if controversial moment in legislative invention and an essential part of the famous New Improved Thinking. It was in fact the theoretical cornerstone in the New Global Order and a real watershed for psychologists. One of my professors used to say, in his famous way, 'Talk is for losers.' He was all for the great de-certification. He supported turning psychology over to the 'nuts-and-bolts guys,' the guys who handle mental illness with chemicals in fifty-gallon drums. But no, it's the psychology of industry itself that we're concerned with. The truth we must acknowledge is that large, complex organizations of ideas, money, physical plants, police infrastructure, and what we once called human practices (or behavior) generate activities that we now refer to more accurately as 'meat tendencies.' It is with these complex organizational tendencies that Industrial Psychology is concerned."

"Give me an example, dear. It's all a little complicated for me." Cecile took a small bite of jellied toast.

"Sure. Nothing simpler. Think of Nikbok. Sports shoes, right? Sneakers. It is, and has been for decades, an Austrian company. Yet its only real market is in the United States, and its factories are on the Pacific Rim and in Mexico. This all makes it a very typical world-industrial organization. The money generated by the company's activities mostly flows and occasionally puddles. As much as possible, they like the money to puddle in Austria. This is all, of course, economics, not psychology. The psychology is elsewhere. Nikbok tells itself, its market, and even its employees that it is actually a very subversive company. It hates conformism. It hates all the drones and the clones. It is about liberation. When you are wearing Nikboks, you may appear another compliant robot, but inside you are taking it all the way, full court, and slamming in the defenseless face of the enemy! This, if you think about it, is an exciting and innovative process. It contains and makes productive its own internal contradictions. Brilliant! Fascinating! But what of the other component? The workers? Aren't they miserable? Underpaid? Of course, they are paid the lowest possible wages, but they are also provided—in the worker communities—with the most exciting opportunities.

They are provided with things they could never find in their dingy, ancestral villages. The girls wear make-up and high heels to work. After work, it's off to the nightclubs where they can drink things through colored straws that return them to the pessimism of pre-social human nature, and they can dance dances like the Calculated Gesture to the New Reality beat of a local synth-band. And it's all part of one intoxicatingly rich and complex system that—at the psychological level—is simply not concerned with 'making tennis shoes,' but then neither is it particularly concerned with what goes on inside an individual human head. It's the psychology of systems that we're interested in."

"If it works so well, why do these systems need psychologists?" Cecile had gotten a bit of jam on her mouth. She searched for it with a fleshy tongue that seemed to Hans to pulse. Hans was so taken with and seduced by her effort that he nearly stuck his own tongue out.

"Well, all systems need analysts, at some point. Nobody else needs to understand the entire scope of the thing, not even the so-called owners, who, from our point of view, are just another aspect of system psychology."

"But why does the system need you?"

"Oh, occasionally things go a little cuckoo."

"Cuckoo?"

"Yeah, pretty cuckoo. Like say the nightlife gets a little carried away in the *barrio*. (For whatever reason, it usually is the workers that create the problems that require psychological help.) Let's say some teenage girls don't show up for work. Let's say they're discovered in a local landfill. That news, especially if it visits the ears of the tennis-shoe-wearing consumer in the States who carries some old-fashioned political notions in his or her individual brain, can cause a tiny vibration which if unchecked can rattle an entire global organism."

"How awful."

"It is potentially destabilizing as all heck. Full industrial neurotic intensity. At its far reach, it is self-destructive if, for instance, Nikbok makes a foolish gesture like reintroducing labor unions as an act of remorse. Or funds a clinic or something."

"And this is where you come in?"

"Right. They ask us to explain."

"Who's they?"

"Authorities."

"And what do you explain?"

"We say, for example, that it's the work of sexual perverts. Then the police round up all of the sexual perverts in the area and they find one to punish. They have a rich heritage of punishing down there. From a human perspective, these punishments are perhaps cruel, but from an industrial psychological perspective, they are in fact health-giving. Punishment of perverts is welcome news to the radicalized patrons of Nikbok tennis shoes in *Los Estados Unidos*. For if their humanitarian concerns are not addressed, they can start to feel what we call a 'clinical and chronic disinclination to participate,' which can mean puddles of un-bought tennis shoes instead of money."

"I see."

"So industry is powerful but it is also vulnerable and subject to all of the doubts and traumas and panics and, yes, depressions of regular humans of times past. Industrial anhedonia, the failure of systems to experience pleasure, is no pretty sight. Lethargic factories, despairing executives. You can practically see the buildings weep. So, we're an important part of what we call global corporate homeostasis or, in an older idiom, 'health,' or, as we say among ourselves, 'lookin' good.'"

"Lookin' good! I'm impressed."

Hans nodded as if to say, "You should be."

"But tell me, Hans, what do you know of sexual perversion?"

Hans looked at Cecile in horror. He was always being taken off-guard by these people. He stormed back as best he could. "I don't need to know anything about sexual perversion beyond the concept. As I explained, that's a matter for the police. We trust the police to know all about it."

Cecile was surely going to reply but didn't because at just that moment, at their side, a voice bellowed, "Oh, so here you are!"

It was Mayor Jesse.

"Well, well," he said, "glad to see ya, glad to see ya."

He looked at Hans and Cecile as if he had in fact caught them *in flagrante*, on the tabletop, Cecile up to her naked rear in the oatmeal.

"Morning, Jesse," Cecile replied, smiling and nodding. She seemed not at all disturbed by his sudden appearance.

The Mayor looked at Hans, his large, ogling, bloodshot blue eyes swimming in rheum. The purple hue of his face seemed to set his head off from his body, as if it were really a fun, detachable doll's head.

"I'm glad to see that you're getting to know the folks here, Mr. Castro. Taking meals, too. You know, nothing makes a family like ritual, and there is no ritual like taking meals together. With good eating habits, you can fit right in up here. And you've already discovered that there are no quality control issues in the lady market here and damned near no competition at this hour of the morning! Hey?" The Mayor pummeled Hans's right shoulder.

"I was just telling Cecile about my study of Industrial Psychology."

"Oh Industrial Psychology, is it? That's a cold subject for mealtimes, for family ritual space, son. Anyhow, what I'm sayin' is, you watch come dinner, hell, lunch if our lovely *fraulein* has lunch, she'll look like the proverbial pork chop with a pack of hounds. The boys here like her. So enjoy her while you can. She's one of the real popular ones. Darned if she isn't. You'll see. Everybody sees. So, enjoy yourself, enjoy yourself."

Cecile plucked a square bite of potato off the tines of her fork, delicately, with her perfectly straight teeth.

13

Hans felt a little better after breakfast. He now knew two things. First, there would in fact be food that he could actually eat. Second, he had made a friend, even if it was a friend that was capable of making anxiety surge through him, not to mention lust, although he didn't know to call it that. Nonetheless, knowing her made Hans feel more confident about the idea of surviving two weeks at The Elixir. If something very disturbing happened with his cousin, he could at least try talking to this—German?—woman. But breakfast and its revelations were only the beginning of "the human touch" prepared for him that bright day.

When he approached his quarters in the Mr. Donut, he could see through the large plate-glass windows that a small crowd of mostly older, if not quite elderly, women bustled inside. They all seemed to be carrying baskets with red-checkered cloths over the top. Seeing Hans approach, they came rushing out as if each wished to be the first to scream, "Surprise! Surprise!" and clutch on to his arm. Hans felt immediate revulsion. He had never been able to endure women, especially women his mother's age, grasping him and expressing any sort of pleasure in his presence. Affection! They were disgusting, those old wrinkled hands. So he merely looked at them stiffly, his attitude full of helplessness. But Hans's discomfort didn't dampen their gushing enthusiasm at all.

One of them gathered herself enough to stop her idiotic bubbling so that she could speak. "Oh Mr. Castorp—you are Mr. Castorp?—we're so glad to meet you. We are from Caring Caravan International, a far-flung business enterprise established to make strange places feel like home in our mobile society, so that everywhere is our home and no place is foreign, no, not even if you were in colorful Kabul, and we are your basket ladies!" Everyone cheered as if they truly rejoiced in this identity. Hans half-expected them to break into some sort of school song, as if this were Spirit Week and they were really determined to win. Then they decided it was time to go inside, into the lobby, where folding chairs, a crock-pot full of warm cider and a platter of cookies and other cellophane-wrapped treats waited. Corporate logos were all over the wall behind the treats as if the people in market development really thought a lot of Hans's potential for snack consumption.

Finally, when everyone was seated, a woman introduced herself. "My name is Aunt Pearl," she said. Hans thought that all of these women could be called Aunt Pearl. They reminded him of the cloning triumphs that his professors were predicting for the retail services industry. In the New America every cashier was to be a perfect cashier. He couldn't help but wonder who would find it a bright idea to clone these Aunt Pearls. "As I explained outside, we are from Caring Caravan International. We welcome newcomers to approximately three thousand towns and cities in the United States and Canada. What we bring, in addition to words of welcome (and our own joy!), is in these baskets." She handed her basket over to Hans. He delicately pulled back the cloth. Given his earlier experiences at The Elixir, he had no idea what to expect to find. He figured he shouldn't expect a warm apple pie. Perhaps it was another bottle of vodka. But haven't we always found that doors, veils, drawers, coverings, anything which hides something else from less than frankly open view, haven't we always found this closing off, this shutting in, this *hiding* to be suspicious, even sinister? Doors, who trusts 'em? On the other side of the door, isn't that your girlfriend having sex with her drama coach? Isn't that your teenage daughter getting it on with the pet collie? Isn't that your uncle pointing his World War Two lugar at his head? Fortunately, all Hans found in fact was a bounty of trial-size containers including: shaving cream, pantyhose, mouthwash, depilatory, shampoo, freeze-dried chicken almondine, and one enormous oatmeal-and-raisin cookie in shrink-wrap. He plucked out the depilatory cream and looked at it in bewilderment. Hans returned it to the basket and Aunt Pearl continued.

"That's all for your use while you're here at The Elixir, no need to return what you don't use. Ordinarily, we would also give you helpful printed materials about the new community—its schools, churches, motor vehicle laws, town government, and maps—but The Elixir doesn't have any of those things. It will soon, though," she beamed optimistically, "if the proposed annexations of nearby Diamond and Eileen go through. Then we'll be the proper county seat, and about time! There's just one more thing, then we'll leave you in peace to go through your goodies." Aunt Pearl looked around at all the other Aunt Pearls as if asking permission for something naughty.

"Oh tell him, tell him," they cried.

"You are also signed on for our most popular service on a special one-week get-acquainted basis: 'Care-ring,' our telephone companion service. We at Caring Caravan International have responded to the pervasive loneliness of our times by creating a telephone service whereby a corporate representative will call twice-a-day at appointed hours just to let you know that we care. Your representative's name is LaCrema Pui Desconsolo, and she's a lovely African-Thai-Mexican-American girl working her way through the Pontiac Academy of Beauty." She opened a glossy brochure. "LaCrema likes poetry of the English Restoration, long walks in the Biological Autonomous Zone, and cream-based desserts." Aunt Pearl handed Hans the full-color brochure. LaCrema was indeed a beautiful young woman, but her face seemed to Hans to shift continuously under his gaze, like a hologram, from one ethnic type to another. She peeked at him over one naked shoulder, the upper slope of a voluptuous breast just showing.

"Thank you very much," said Hans.

"We will need a credit card number if you ever want to hear from LaCrema again after week one." Aunt Pearl beamed as if this were, for obscure reasons, awfully good news. "Now, Mr. Castorp, we have one last treat for you. A special message from one of The Elixir's smallest residents. Our own Timmy!"

Out from among the sea of calico skirts came a boy, maybe twelve-years-old.

Timmy came forward and addressed Hans. "Mr. Castorp, my tale is not a pleasant one. I still do not know what it was that I did wrong. I will try to explain. When I was little, my father was a mystery to me. He worked late every night. My mother was always sad because Daddy didn't come home. When he was home, we hid from him and his temper. I felt unloved and shut out by my father, but I hid these negative emotions. I dealt with anger and frustration by stuffing them down. I stuffed them and stuffed them." At this point, Timmy spun weirdly to his left, away from Hans, carried away by his dramatic stuffing gestures, as if he were a little windup toy that had hit an uneven spot on the floor. Aunt Pearl took him by the shoulders and turned him back toward Hans.

Timmy continued. "Only recently, with the help of Mr. Ricky and others here at The Elixir, have I realized that for many years I had blocked out horrible things. I blocked out these memories. With guidance, I remembered that when I was five, my father left the family to live with the fancy woman with breasts. He refused to give me any money in spite of the fact that he was so rich because the fancy woman with breasts bought him a bank. But when I visited him, he said, 'I'm ashamed of the way you dress, Timmy. You dress like a poor person. I don't want to be seen with you looking like that!' So he gave me some nice new clothes with creases right in them. They put the creases in at the store. And then the woman with fancy breasts helped me put my new clothes on. I was so happy! I wanted to show Mommy. But when I went home, Daddy made me take the clothes off and leave them behind because he thought I'd just ruin them at Mommy's 'slut shack.' My daddy and the fancy breasts with a woman always laughed at our poor slut shack. I had to put my clothes with creases in them away in an empty dresser drawer before I could leave."

By the time Timmy was done talking, tears were flowing down Hans's cheek. That was such a sad story! Hans caught Timmy's eye, as if to communicate sympathy, but Timmy scowled in reply. All the

Aunt Pearls then boiled to the surface of the room and prepared to leave. For a moment, in their frantic scurrying, it appeared Timmy might be overlooked. Hans's feelings of sympathy were quickly erased by the fear that they might say, "Oh, he's yours now! He stays right here with you! That's part of the deal. Don't expect us to take him! What kind of young man are you? That's a funny business, to be sure!" Timmy must have seen this change-of-heart expressed in Hans's features, for he came directly over as if he had something private to share with Hans. He looked up at Hans, and tugged at his coat sleeve. He said, "I'm all right, Jack. Don't kid yourself. They pay me to say that crap." Somehow, unlikely as it may seem, Timmy managed to shove his face right into Hans's as he concluded, "And I don't give fuck-all about you or your kind!"

14)

After the women from the Caring Caravan had gone, Hans retreated
to his room. He was over-stimulated in the extreme. He needed some
downtime. He sat in an armchair and soon realized that he was staring at a TV set. Now, he hadn't noticed before that there was a TV
set in the room. He looked it over. Could the Aunt Pearls have left it
behind for him? Or had it been there the whole time and he simply
hadn't noticed? But now that he had noticed it, he didn't know quite
what to do. He felt uncomfortably self-conscious. It was almost as if
the TV were looking at him. And, if Hans were right, it didn't seem
to think much of what it saw. This particular TV was of no specific
manufacture, was a purely generic TV, straight entry level, with no
controls at all except on/off. It seemed to dare him to turn it on.
And why should he not turn it on? It was in the room for him, after
all. It was there for his pleasure. It was there for exactly this sort of
downtime, away from the rigors of the Cure.

Hans sat undecided for several minutes. Finally, because he was
an American and Americans cannot possibly choose not to turn on
a TV, he got up and approached the thing. He extended his hand as
if he were going to touch an animal he had never touched before, or

as if he had never touched an animal before. He turned the TV on. Nothing. Hans was relieved. But then he began to investigate why it hadn't gone on. Was it plugged in? Was the cable properly attached? Had a fuse blown? Was there any electrical hook-up to the building? Did anything at all work in this dumb donut room? He concentrated on these questions, determined to fix what he simultaneously feared would work. He turned the TV off. Only then did he hear the dim base line. Then the crooning vocal. Finally an entire orchestra. LET'S FLY AWAY, LET'S FLY, LET'S FLY AWAY! It was the loudest music Hans had ever heard. JUST SAY THE WORD AND WE'LL BEAT THE BIRDS DOWN TO ACAPULCO BAY! It was all erupting beneath him.

Hans turned the TV back on but the deafening music persisted. He pushed the power button repeatedly, panicked. Anxiety seeped from Hans like tears. IT'S PERFECT FOR A FLYING HONEYMOON, THEY SAY. He began pacing, holding his head. He knew this song. He knew this song from somewhere. He associated it with morning and coffee and the clinking of coffee spoons against a coffee cup. The smell of the morning's first cigarette. Terrifying. SO COME FLY WITH ME . . . He had to figure out where the music was coming from . . . PACK UP LET'S FLY AWAY! He went to the back of his room and opened a door there. It led to a narrow passageway lined with cloth mops, rags, buckets and jugs of bleach. On the left was another door marked "No Admittance Employees Only." Hans tried the door but it was locked. He banged loudly on the door and the music stopped.

Mystery solved, he thought. I have a neighbor.

15

Hans was beginning to think he didn't much like this room in which books hid bottles and the TV seemed to open out to other hidden realms. Never mind Aunt Pearl's efforts to make him feel welcome. Such a welcome had its own strangeness. What else did this room hide? Hans decided to investigate the other books in the room. Would they all contain bottles of cheap vodka? Would they have dull stories about boys and their pencils? Or would they reveal other unsuspected things? Here was one called *The Big Book of Despair*. Hans opened it carefully but found it quite whole. No bottle was buried in it. There was a little sticker on the inside cover. The sticker was brittle and yellow and the adhesive had leaked through the paper staining it brown. But you could still read: "Distributed with best wishes by the Society for the Redress of Universal Despair." The first story in the book was called "The Dog of Despair."

Within each person live two dogs. Both dogs are strong and fight for a person's heart. The person chooses which dog will be the stronger by deciding which dog to feed.

One of the dogs is called the Dog of Despair. The other is called I'm Happy. Our-Father-who-art-on-the-couch is constantly throwing the dog called Despair large chunks of raw meat. Hog corpses. Jowls. Shanks. I'm Happy, on the other hand, is on a starvation diet. When I'm Happy tries to walk, he can only move a front paw and whimper. He's so weak. But he takes it well, he's smiling, because he's The Dog of I'm Happy. The idea that I'm Happy could ever be as big as the Dog of Despair makes the Dog of Despair laugh in doggy mirth. He rolls over on his doggy back and kicks out his cruel legs and roars with the impossibility of it. Still, just the idea that I'm Happy wants to be fed, and could be fed, might still have the strength to eat, makes him nervous. For until the Dog of I'm Happy is just completely gone, there will always be the possibility that Our-Father-who-art-in-possession-of-the-remote-control-television-device could theoretically feed him and stay within the stretchy laws of dharmic possibility. So he takes a long, serious, sidelong, hungry look at the weak puddle that is the body of the Dog of I'm Happy. A formerly dim doggy corpuscle flashes into fire. He thinks, I should just go eat the Dog of I'm Happy and be done with it. Then I'm Happy would not only not be a threat to the food that I receive by the wheelbarrow load, he would become the food itself. He would be the food that he doesn't get! Funny! Funny! The Dog of Despair thought this was unbelievably funny and poetic and in dog terms totally brilliant! The Dog of I'm Happy would itself become part of the food that makes the Dog of Despair stronger. Get it? The multiple ironies came at him in large numbers. He turned them this way and that like multifaceted Milk-Bones. Then he rolled over and laughed, twitching his doggy legs in the air like a comical Hindu dog god. Then he rolled back to his feet and looked blackly dead ahead. He focused on nothing except this serious intent. He was going to do it. Now. Strike while the iron is hot and the hour is at hand. Or, as his dog buddies said, "pounce while the bunny is lame." He just hoped that the crunching of the larger bones wouldn't wake Our Father. He rose. He took the first momentous step. He would be the All Dog now. The Everything Dog. The Dog of Ubiquity. Yes. But then another thought came to him. "I will be Big and I will be Bigger, but Big as compared to what? Bigger than what?" That was his awful, chilling thought. Was there a dog of Mediocre Feelings around? A Dog of More or Less? Or a dog of Comic Coups, perhaps? Or Painful Fuck-ups? Anything would do. But he thought not. He sat down and stared off into a bizarre canine space and became absorbed in a despairing meditation on his impossible quandary. He was beginning to understand why they called him the Dog of Despair. This was some sad shit. It was impossible to avoid a simple conclusion: he, the big strong Dog of Despair, was dependent on the puny little bitch kitty Dog of I'm Happy. The thought disgusted him.

Then the most deeply disturbing thought: the arrival of the *thought* of dependency is not dependency itself, for he has always been dependent without knowing it. No, the arrival of the understanding of his dependency is, in fact, the arrival of his failure! His defeat! Which has been sleeping in him stupidly the whole time! And he could not see it because he was the stupid, beer drinking, frisbee playing, jingle-ball chasing Dog of Despair. His "brilliant idea" of what would make him superlative, fully realized, has in fact made him fully realized: he is the DOG OF DESPAIR.

He lies down as if for the last time.

At some point in the sad later, he feels a slight, painful sensation in his hind legs. This sensation doesn't really hurt, but it is enough to make him lift his ponderous dog skull and look back. He sees that the Dog of I'm Happy has somehow managed to drag his lax corpse over and is beginning to nibble on his hind feet. Already there is a thin gloss of blood on his black dog lips. The Dog of Despair thinks that the blood looks like lipstick and that's just perfect for that little pussy bitch kitty. He laughs. Fuckin' perfect, man! I'm Happy, seeing Despair's look, grins sickly and shrugs his shoulders as if to say, "What am I supposed to do? I'm hungry."

The Dog of Despair puts his dog skull back down on the ground and groans. Then he has his last thought before he bleeds to death through his now chewed off hind-foot: "It's a dog-eat-dog world, man," and he makes one of those little shuddering laughs that dogs make while dreaming.

Later, the Dog of I'm Happy sits at Our Father's side watching boxing on TV on a Saturday afternoon. It's daytime but the blinds are closed. I'm Happy has been licking an old plate of fudge all afternoon. The fudge is so old and hard that it has actually cut his tongue. Dogs do not know how to stop the bleeding when their tongues bleed. They also do not know how to stop licking fudge once they have started. But he enjoyed the taste of the salty blood mixed with the sweet of the candy and imagined in some dim way that it might actually be nutritious for him. I'm Happy has been watching an old commercial for a beer called Hamms. Hamms beer. It is from the Land of Sky-blue Water. It is the "beer refreshing." Hamms the beer refreshing. The commercial confuses I'm Happy. A bear paddles a canoe. There is a beaver. Smoke signals. What does it mean? It is all very contradictory in his dog brain. How does this commercial make people drink beer? Then the boxing match comes back and the black and white humans are hitting each other, then the beer commercial with the bear in the canoe again. The same one. Same words. Land of Sky-blue Water. Huh. Huh. He meditates on it, continuing to lick the fudge with his bleeding tongue.

Our Father loves I'm Happy. He says, "I have a surprise for you, buddy. Come on!" And he leads the dog, who is barely able to move, so contentedly fat has he become, to a large cardboard box back in the pantry. He lifts I'm Happy up to look over the edge. There is a puppy. The puppy gets up on his little weak puppy legs and whines and wags his tiny puppy tail. "I thought you might be lonesome since you lost your pal. So I got you a new friend. He's little now, but we'll feed him and pretty soon he'll be big like you." I'm Happy feels a sinking feeling. He's beginning to wonder if this sinking feeling is what is meant by the word "happy."

16

The following idea occurred to Hans: he had nothing to do in this place except wait for the next meal. "One meal at a time" was his new motto. The next meal always promised at least to sever him from the awfulness of the events he associated with the previous meal. On the other hand, he was beginning to see that each new meal brought with it a new arrangement of mostly terrifying experiences. Actually, he didn't know what to hope for. He tried to sit quietly, but in his mind he was repeatedly leaping from his chair and literally running through a wall. He was becoming desperate for a dim old feeling he associated with living in a college dormitory. The banality of neutral comfort. He longed for it. Potato chip days. Evenings alone watching the Penis Comedy Channel.

At last it was just about noon and Hans began walking toward the re-tooled Daffy's. He tried to think of the comfort that a grilled cheese sandwich might offer. At the same time, Hans was thinking that he might see Cecile again. There, his thoughts were anything but complacent. She caused in him a frightening little flickering pulse which in anyone else we would call lust but that in our Hans we had better just call more confusion. He had made up his mind that if he saw her at lunch he was going to . . . touch her hand. Yes. That was it. He would reach across the table on some pretext and press his fingers on her hand. He couldn't imagine how she would react to such an outlandish thing. He thought she would probably just blast off.

It seemed to Hans that Cecile was really out of place here. She looked like a woman from the 1940s. She had auburn hair, for example. Exactly! Her hair was brown with reddish highlights but you could only think of calling it "auburn." She wore her hair parted on one side and curling over her brow. Very lovely. Loose, but not so loose that it would get in the way of . . . jitterbugging! That was her exactly! She was like the gorgeous jitterbugging girls of the 1940s that he'd seen on TV.

That was her filthiness.

This word shocked Hans. Filthy. Yes, now that he thought of it, she was sadly filthy. Flirty. Dirty. Suddenly he saw her lifting her gray, pleated skirt in a hidden aisle, back in the musty social science stacks of the library. Her thighs were dimpled but perfectly formed. "Come, little Hans. Research!"

"I want, I want," muttered Hans, "a grilled cheese sandwich."

But he would get no grilled cheese sandwich that day. On Daffy's door was a hastily-scrawled sign, apparently done with a broken crayon. This was certainly Teddy's handiwork. It read: "Lunch cancelled. See below." Hans looked down and found a large bulk-shipping box full of one-serving containers of freeze-dried turkey tetrazini. "Remove paper cover. Fill tray with boiling water. Wait three minutes. Serve immediately." But where would he get boiling water?

"Cold water works, too. It just takes a little longer," said a voice to his side.

Hans turned to find his Cousin Ricky sitting on a block of con-crete to the side of an always-empty newspaper vending machine.

"Ricky. You startled me."

"Sorry, old boy."

Hans retrieved his pulse. "Why is there no lunch today?"

Ricky got up, hands in the front pockets of his jeans, and walked slowly toward Hans. "Guess somebody decided it wasn't important or they couldn't be bothered, or there'd always be more lunches so no biggee."

Hans was outraged. "Well, you'd think there'd be some announce-ment."

"What do you call that?" Ricky gestured toward Teddy's sign.

"I call that inadequate. What if someone were really hungry or were just counting on lunch? Is lunch not an important meal in these parts?"

Ricky took Hans by the elbow and began moving him gently away. "You learn not to count on things here, Cousin. It's better that way." Ricky opened one of the boxes of turkey tetrazini by its top, as if it were a box of Cracker Jacks, and poured some into his palm. "People learn to be self-reliant here. You learn not to need other people. It's part of the Cure. You see, don't you?" He threw back a handful of the freeze-dried stuff. Hans could hear his molars crushing it.

"Where is everyone else? No one seems to have taken any of this junk."

"They're probably with the Mayor down at the Quonset hut."

It's hard to say why, but this seemed to enrage Hans even more than the cancellation of lunch (which, we should remember, is also the defer-ral of his fantasy with Cecile; the disappointed lover is written all over his disproportionate emotions). Nonetheless, enraged he suddenly was. "Are you telling me that these sick people are, first, missing their lunch and then spending this lovely afternoon in a building with no windows with that awful Mayor character?" Hans slapped his thigh and threw his head back. "It isn't good enough," he said violently, "it just isn't good enough to calmly proclaim, just calmly," his words trailed off in a fit of laughter that seized and overcame him, "that this is a place of cure and then," a profound, body-shaking laughter shut his eyes, "and then give you freeze-dried turkey, or whatever this stuff is, and shut you up in a Quonset hut. My God! My God! People have to eat! People have to eat food! Real food!"

Ricky thumped his cousin once, with his index finger, on his protruding sternum. Hans looked up fearfully, sputtering through his laughter.

"Keep quiet," Ricky said sternly. "There are people here for whom The Elixir is a most sacred and serious place. If you carry on like this, you won't stay long. And you do wish to stay, don't you?"

"Yes, yes I do," replied Hans. And in fact he was already convinced that he did wish to stay.

Hans looked over at the Quonset hut. It was maybe twenty yards away at the end of a cracked concrete walk. The concrete reflected an intense early afternoon heat. Hans couldn't imagine what it was like inside the hut. A good place for baking bricks. His hilarity was gone, but it still seemed unbelievable to him that human beings would willingly agree to congregate there. He could just hear the strangest laughter, muffled and distant, coming from the hut. There was some sort of strange *bonhomie* going on in there. Some sort of general regaling.

"Ricky," said our sober Hans, "tell me. What goes on in there really?"

Ricky faced the hut, but his look was far-away. His expression seemed to say, "I could tell you now. I could tell you exactly, but you wouldn't understand."

"And if everyone is there, why aren't you there? Why aren't *we* there?"

"Eventually, old boy, you'll spend a lot of time in there." Ricky's face seemed for the first time to hold a human emotion other than his habitual removed, knowing amusement. He looked almost sad. Maybe it was compassion. Hans thought, for a moment, that Ricky's eyes might even be teary. He continued somberly, "That's where you belong. With the other men. But that time is not yet. You're not ready. Don't rush things. You're a young man. You have plenty of time."

Hans nodded, not sure whether he should feel reassured or threatened. He looked again at the hut. It looked as far away as a dwarf nebula. Far away though it seemed, the noisy, echoing sounds were perfectly audible. Someone was yelling, his voice above the crowd. It was the Mayor. Hans thought he heard him say, "Niggers don't count here!" There was a general, amused roar of approval and confirmation.

Then a real racket began, a screaming such as Hans had never heard in his life, and then a shriek full of horror and rebellion and pain. A gruesome sort of begging accented it all. Then it became a dull and hollow sound, as though the hut had sunk down into the middle of the earth. Finally, an outburst of laughter and someone yelled, "Touchdown!"

Hans turned back to his cousin. He wanted to ask Ricky what this was all about. Were they just watching football in there? But the little, nodding smile on his cousin's face told him that, no, he heard nothing, or would not acknowledge hearing anything. Then Ricky's smile turned into a large, amused laugh.

"Oh Hans, you tickle me. You are trying so hard, old boy, to understand, aren't you? Watching your face when you think is like watching a very busy construction site from the top of a hill. All these little people are scurrying, doing the most absurd things."

Ricky put his arm around Hans's shoulder and led him away. "Let's take a walk," he said.

There was a path leading out behind the restaurant. It went past a jarring mix of fresh garbage and discarded junk; there was the strangest pile of old metal french-fry baskets piled up like an abstract civic sculpture, like something Chicago would pay a fortune for. Incongruous and verdant clumps of sweet-smelling honeysuckle and unmanaged forsythia threatened to overtake the whole thing. Quickly, the two cousins penetrated between the nearest slag heaps and into a little narrow pass. Hans wasn't sure whether to call it a valley or an alley. It all looked very foreign and weird to him. It looked like pictures he'd seen of rocky outcroppings and peaks above alpine tree lines where only lichens grew, clinging fiercely to blasted granite. But he didn't see lichens, and the dwarfish scale made the alpine comparison absurd.

At the very base of the slag, however, was a strange vegetable growth. As they walked into this odd valley, Hans repeatedly asked himself what this odd vegetation could be. They weren't flowers, or weeds, or grasses, or bushes such as he'd ever seen. They looked like tiny trees. But what did he know? He was a city boy.

Ever observant, Ricky noticed Hans's intrigue. "They're bonsai, old boy. Nature's finest." He took advantage of the pause to take his flask from his jacket pocket and take a sip that said, "That's a fact."

"What on earth do you mean, 'bonsai'? I thought bonsai was a technique that the Japanese invented. A way of cultivating miniature plants in containers."

"Right as rain, Cousin. But take a look." Ricky bent and yanked one of the little knotted and black-dark oaks from the rocky dirt. The roots stuck firm, so he tore the plant at its base. "Here's the proof. A mature oak tree. The rocky conditions here, combined with trace toxins from the old mines, and the frequent acid rain we get here since Illinois became a perfect little terrarium, have created an environment ideal for these stunted but, I think you will agree, charming trees."

Hans bent down to look at another. Yes, there was something cute about the little buggers. This one was a little maple. Here was a little hedge of them, standing like a rough fringe along the path, ready for the weed-whacker. He stood. Then he had a strong thought: "But these are no damned adequate replacement for proper trees." Hans might have done something more with this sudden, pure resentment, but they were interrupted by the arrival of a strange man—cane in hand, an elegant cloth hat perched on the side of his head—strolling back toward downtown.

17

It was hard to say how old their interloper was. He gave the immediate impression of youthfulness—plenty of smile and swagger—but the gray in the wavy hair at his temples said he was close to forty-five. He dressed in black, a baggy suit gone very shiny at the elbows. There were small holes and larger abrasions at the knees, as if he'd once slid into second base in this suit. It was the kind of suit that you couldn't get new; you had to buy it at a thrift store. Still, the overall effect was an appeal to elegance (even if a soiled elegance). He carried a cane, wore a striking jewel-green silk tie (complete with gravy stain), and draped his great coat over his shoulders. He reminded Hans of the street musicians, expelled from all cities with a population over 500,000 by one of the provisions of the Civic Purgation Act. They now roamed like troubadours from place to place frequently ending up at mid-size university towns like Downstate playing their disintegrating guitars and waggling their impoverished heads, all blue cheer and green tambourines. People still called them "hippies." Hans only knew that they made him nervous and being nervous made him want to pretend they weren't there. They made him want to go back to his dorm room, empty all his dirty clothes out of the hamper, and climb inside.

The man stopped before them and stood smiling. He's quite nervy, Hans thought, to intrude on our walk. Or maybe just crazy, like those other street people. A smile that was almost mocking crisped the corners of the man's mouth. His presence immediately reorganized the two cousins.

But, as Hans might have known, Ricky was familiar with him. "Hans, may I present our distinguished colleague, Professor Feeling. Professor Feeling, my cousin Hans Castorp from Downstate."

Feeling extended a long and bony hand. "A very great pleasure to meet you, young man. I have heard of you well before I ever set eyes on you. Here at The Elixir you have a great number of devoted admirers." He paused, staring at Hans as if at some slowly evolving but fascinating geological phenomenon. "A very great pleasure to meet you indeed."

Hans looked over at his cousin who raised his eyebrows in order to say, "Don't look at me. I never said a word."

But Feeling missed nothing and took him up. "Ah, not so quick, my friends, it's completely true. Your cousin has spread the saga of your vast accomplishments." He turned a yellowish hand toward the sky. "In your presence, one could almost forget where one is."

"That's very nice of you to say."

"Oh, don't mistake me. I'm not saying it."

"Pardon me?"

"And what kind of sentence has the Mayor knocked you down for? Don't tell me you got off easy! First time offender? Let me guess. Six months with stipulated liquid remedy? The old solvent recuperator, eh?"

Hans was alarmed by this so-called Professor's assumptions. "I think, Professor Feeling, that you aren't aware of the purpose for my visit. I'm here to see my cousin for a strictly limited period of time. I certainly can't stay. Not only do I have a real job at Caterpillar in Peoria, but I have job applications for my next move floating across Central Illinois."

"Caterpillar! Magnificent! Just the name! Its aura! Blinding! And 'next move,' you say? Stalwart young man that you are! Next stop the empyrean, eh? Oh, he's just like you said, Ricky, the little engine that could. A rarity in this air, I'll say."

Hans looked at Ricky again. Little engine?

"My point, Professor, is simply, that anything beyond two weeks is intolerable."

"Intolerable! Ricky, he is so fine! A true gem of our higher education system! He has (how shall I put it?) DICTION! That's how I shall put it." But then the Professor took a very pointed, sidelong, and dubious look at Hans. "So let me understand," he continued, "nothing for *you* to recover from, eh? You're just right as rain. You've 'got it all together, man,' as we used to say." He gave his shoulders a grinding turn as if to emphasize that he had nothing but contempt for the idea of someone "having it together."

"May I be so bold as to ask what you, the man-of-no-ills, do when you are not generously visiting family in places for the less fortunate?"

Hans frowned. He suspected by this time that at The Elixir any candor would almost certainly be used against him. But he couldn't see a polite way around stating at least the basic facts. So he said, "I have just recently finished my studies in Industrial Psychology at Downstate University."

Feeling reared back, his eyes widening, as if to say, "I am impressed."

"Industrial Psychology! You have risen in my estimation, young man! And you were already bumping your head against the very vaulted dome of the sky, in my opinion. How distinguished! But tell me, what is this Industrial Psychology about?" Then with a weary smile, "The condensed version, if you please."

"It's not a simple thing," said Hans evasively, desperate to beg off the subject, sure that he would only reveal himself as a charlatan if he were obliged to say more. "It's not something that I can tell you about briefly."

Ricky nodded and smiled at his cousin's side, enjoying the theater, amused by Hans's tepid response, anticipating Feeling's rejoinder.

"I see. I'm sure that the demands on a man in your profession are enormous. I'm sure that it is best not to have too clear an idea of them. It might take away one's courage. It's no joking matter, is it? I know that for myself, although what I do is not anything near so glamorous as 'Industrial Psychology,' even I know that when I'm asked about my profession, I often find it best to reply, 'I am really fit only for doing nothing at all.' Which is no lie! For my profession—I can tell you, you'll understand, you're the sort who understands—is this: I am a conduit."

"A conduit?"

"Yes, a high-grade channel of energy." Feeling paused and reached into the breast pocket of his suit, retrieving a slim stainless steel flask identical to Ricky's and emblazoned with the large red E for Elixir and beneath that the inscription "Life Is Recovery." In retrieving the flask he inadvertently pulled out a large greenish crystal at the end of a leather necklace. Hans's eyes froze on it. For a moment he thought he could see, fixed within the emerald green, a tiny fetus.

Sensing Hans's stare, Feeling took the crystal gently in his hand. "Ah. You've seen my little crystal. My little key to the eons." He took a vigorous pull on the flask.

Hans did not really want to know anything about this crystal. By this point, his nervous system was shot. He was soaked in dread. Anything which was less than completely familiar (and in this place even his hands looked a little alien) filled him with anxiety. In short, Hans did not really want to know anything about this crystal.

"Ah! You wish to know what it is, perhaps? Yes? It is intriguing, isn't it? Well, let me tell you." Feeling lifted the crystal and held it to his forehead, directly between his eyes. Then he removed the leather necklace and held the crystal at arm's length. It looked like calcified lime Jell-O in which a human embryo floated, curled like a pinkie finger.

Feeling continued in his role as the maestro of mystery. "Each of us," he pronounced, "has the infinite power of the universe within himself." He looked to Hans as if he expected the wildest sort of congratulation for this insight. He got only Hans's half-mortified blankness. Feeling continued, undeterred, "In the beginning, my young friend, the universe was in a pure state of energy." He waved his hands in a ludicrous imitation of oscillating energy waves, which caused him to teeter a bit drunkenly backwards, nearly loosing his balance. "It was a seething mass of energy. Then came the big BANG," he shouted, his arms exploding outward, Hans retreating away from the blast. "Now here comes the tricky part. The bang created stars, and those little dynamos created what we call 'heavy matter.' And what is heavy matter? We are! We are made of the same stuff as stars!

"But the purest creation of the stars is crystal. Like this one that I wear. A crystal is a condensed star, a star whose energy has collapsed and collapsed back onto itself producing this luster. Understand this: crystal is the fundamental structure of creation. It provides a basic connection between us and the mineral kingdom. The energy of the crystal is potentially *your* energy. And for what?" Feeling pounced. "To heal you of your pain!"

Hans spun back from this claim. He felt a little dizzy. Like a mesmerist, Feeling dangled the little green crystal before him. Hans saw again the tiny fetus and this time he was so close that he could also see that the fetus had an even tinier red dot on his chest, near its heart. It was as if it had been perforated through its chest with a needle and a little drop of blood had leaked to the surface.

"Why are you in so much pain, young man!? Come on, out with it!"

But Hans could not out with anything. He felt as if he, too, had been perforated, only through the forehead.

Kindly, Professor Feeling tucked his crystal back into his shirt. Then he spoke calmly. "Many people, dear boy, have vital spiritual experiences while gazing into the stone. They are in the nature of emotional displacements and rearrangements. In fact, I have been trying to produce some such emotional rearrangement within you." He smiled headlong at Hans. "I must acknowledge, however, that I have never been successful with a boy of your description."

18)

Like the Mayor and the Reverend Boyle, Professor Feeling felt obliged to narrate. To explain. While the Mayor had his council meetings and the Reverend his little discourses, the Professor fancied himself some sort of camp counselor. He took a particular interest in the children of The Elixir, perhaps because he hoped through them to make the future his own. Or perhaps it was simply his conviction that he was a child too. Oddly, he claimed the future through memory. He felt a strong responsibility for the past.

He crystallized memory through stories he told to the next generation of The Elixir on summer nights, around a campfire of scrap particleboard and chunks of PVC outside the Quonset hut. The burning PVC created a spectacular blue-green flame that delighted the children. Dozens of kids like Teddy and Timmy, their faces smeared with the soil of disturbed urchin-being, would sit and watch the fire catch facets of the greenish amulet that the Professor wore about his neck. The Professor would then see the amulet reflected back as jaundiced sparkles in each pale little eye. His amulet twinkled and moved among the children as if it were a mossy Tinker Bell dangling from his neck.

He always began with a formulaic introduction.

"Hello, little ones on the Beginners Path." Feeling liked to affect a brogue when he spoke to the children, but it was a poorish brogue because he grew up in nearby Kankakee. Of course, the kids didn't know any better and, for them, it provided a weird sliver of exotic authenticity. They'd have been disappointed if Feeling spoke "regular."

"My name is Feeling and I am a Toxic Adult Child just as you are Toxic Children. Someday you will grow up to be Toxic Adult Children. But we will all always be children. It is as inevitable as the strange change of weather. Little Jennifer, you and your mommy dig barbiturates. Jamal's mother snorts concoctions of heroin and crack. And Winnifred, oh honey, it's strange I know, your daddy likes the rush of mainlining environmental hormone mimickers. PCBs dissolved in Wild Turkey. You haven't been high till you've had your DNA stalk shaken like a peach tree. That's what we call a baseline buzz.

"I want to tell you another of my life stories tonight. This one is not about such an old life. When you're lit, when you're burning bright, when your veins are incandescent with Substance, you can get right through one life, torch it like an arson accelerating through a cheap apartment complex, and get on with the next one. Because we've got thousands of them to burn, children, till we can get to the Pure Flame, that Flame which leaves not the slightest ash. So, best to Dope the Flame, children, put something in the blood to make it burn bright. As for the tears, if you're really blessed, they'll ignite, too, and run like torchbearers down your face.

"My life was typical of any child in the America of that period. I was born the son of the president of a large advertising agency. At a very early age, I was Selling Time. We take this for granted now. But once Selling Time was an extraordinary thing: the last commodity frontier. Compared to it, Selling Space was a snap. I won't even mention Selling Things, something we'd left to our servants many years before.

"But, of course, you don't see Time as something to sell unless you have Shattering Clarity. Today you can get that ready-to-go in a tiny ampule that you break under your nose. Or load up for the whole day with those suppositories that the Mayor loves, the ones that look like space rockets. All thanks to the alert chemical engineers in Darhest, Louisiana, Substance Valhalla. But way back then, I could gain a solid sense of life's drift only by drinking quantities of single malt scotch. Oh, yes, it was a shattering clarity, but it was also redundant and inefficient. You had to drink so darned much of the stuff. Not that I minded at the time.

"At sixteen, I moved to New Orleans where cocktail parties were the order of the day. There, I made the personal discovery of little paper napkins, pastel glasses in which our olives swam, and skirts with slits up the back. That's when I met Roque. 'No hay problema,' he said, because he liked a transvestite who wore her skirt so short you could see her penis. I was really in a terrific state. There was absolutely nothing wrong. So I was considerably amazed when I woke up one day in the Booby Hatch. I was sprawled on a concrete floor. I said to the orderly, 'Please. For God's sake. Do something charitable for once in your life. Do something smacking of intelligence. Do something that will serve to humanize conduct in the contemporary world. Help often comes in unexpected forms, you know. So surprise me! Get me my tumbler of bourbon. My initials are Scotch-taped to the neck. It's been waiting here for me for many years. I think its time is ripe.'

"And that nice boy brought me decanters and even a bowl of salted peanuts in case I was hungry. I spent some of my happiest days in the Hatch, as we hilariously called it. Gentlemen would come by and we would have sipping contests under the spreading oaks. To get me back inside at night, they'd have to tip the grounds to set me rolling.

"In short, that life was a bed of proverbial roses. I swallowed life in pill form. I did so many things. I generated a new center for human affairs, arguing that the children could take care of themselves. They could get themselves ready if going to school was so darned important. On top of that, I learned to fine-tune a four-barrel carburetor. Those nice boys showed me. I made sure the fuel ran extra rich. If something did come along to upset me, I'd drop a dime in the box and call somebody to deliver a case of McDougal's Quail Egg Ale. And don't forget the spoon!

"It was at this time that I began telling my friends, 'Be still, and know that I am God.' To this day, my many friends and acquaintances from that period send me cards and small trinkets of gratitude in thanks for the revelation.

"Finally, when I was twenty-two, I visited my doctor and said, 'Doc, I've got symptoms. I graduated at the top of my class. Women follow me around like I've been dipped in a vat of ambergris. I regularly appear on lists of America's most powerful men. It's intriguing to me, because to the best of my recollection I never leave my room. Could this mean that I am an alcoholic?'

"And he looked me up and down and said, 'No, you're not.'

"I was stunned. 'Then why, for goodness sake, haven't you told me so during all these years?'

"'I couldn't be sure. The line between an alcoholic and a person of spirit is not always clear. It's a crazy wisdom, so it's easy to make mistakes. But it became clear to me during your last chest x-ray that you are in fact the next incarnation of the Revlon Lama.'

"'The Revlon Lama? Really? Those nice perfume people?'

"'Exactly. Unhappily, the present Revlon Lama is only half your age and in wonderful health. You're a bit early.'

"I had to admit to myself that he was right. He had cut through delusion. Only by being confronted by the ecstasy of my own enlightened state could I accept the label 'Revlon Lama.'

"My story has a happy ending, if this wasn't happy enough. My drinking was declining precipitously. My friends were worried. The boys at the fraternity house were disgusted with me. They suggested that I marry because there is nothing like a wife to make a guy drink his fair share. And the next thing I knew, I was married.

"She had the most astonishing contempt for me. I would spend the day collecting nodes of celestial wonderment in a tiny indecipherable script on a yellow legal tablet. She spent the day thrashing kindergartners. When she came home, she would say, 'Wash the dishes for Christ's sake. You call collecting nodes of celestial wonderment in a tiny indecipherable script working? My father worked! He re-licked dried or loosened stamps for the United States Postal Service! I don't call being a pseudo-hemi-demi-semi-deity working.'

"'Elspeth,' I said, calmly as I might, 'Elspeth, dear, this rage is bootless.' That always ticked her off because she had no idea what 'bootless' meant. I had found the word stuck to one of my celestial nodes. 'Darling, I'm doing what my Higher Power has instructed me to do.' At which point she dissolved in an incomprehensible rage.

"Toward the end of that life, Elspeth and I had two close friends. We played cards together and drank great barrels of Picket Line Beer, produced in Gettysburg. You recall, perhaps, the holographic label? When you tipped the bottle, the bodies of the Confederate dead rolled into a mass grave. Naturally, I had an affair with the wife. Betrayal makes sex delicious, children.

"For example, one day the four of us were driving in their dingy Toyota in the dark of a corn-infested countryside. My lover, Belle, was a waitress by day, drunk by night. She drifted down the years into jail. Only when I had my hand down her pants could she be said to understand anything. Because my hand could cause her crotch to glow like a crab nebula. So on this night while my friend and Elspeth sat in the front seat and chatted about whatever stupid thing they might chat about, Belle leaned forward between the seats and made as if to join their conversation. She asked them what life in Cleveland, Ohio, was all about. And did they believe in the power of suggestion to breach the present indulgent cynicism over the state of nations? My friend and Elspeth shared the belief that they carried the world's troubles on their shoulders. Of course, they did not. I carried the world's troubles in the little plastic photo holders in my wallet. But their delusion was nothing less than useful from my perspective. For while they drove and talked and the gas gauge rose and fell like a wounded bird, I plunged a finger sodden and radiant with the bituminous mist chakra into and around Belle's swollen clitoris. In a whisper, I promised her a special bottle of Samsara Irish

Rye if she moaned into my wife's ear when she came. Her convulsing shoulders nearly knocked the little Toyota off the road.

"And do you know what Belle said after she came? She said, 'Does anyone know the cure for the hiccups?'

"I laugh to see such sport, kids! Okay, that's it for tonight. I'll tell you the story of another one of my lives at a later time. Now off to bed."

So saying, the children did rise and boil about his feet.

19

Speaking and speaking, his voice a shock wave which shocks, loosens and readjusts the universe's spinal cord, Professor Feeling circled about the cousins where the three of them have met on the obscure path leading out of downtown. Or perhaps he was just a sort of spiritual sheep dog, circling, gathering, yipping, "Oooh, la la! Sweet sweet!" he said. At last, like a sling that one twirls round the head, he finally let go, flinging them back toward The Elixir. Their so-called walk was apparently done. "Ah, let us go then, the three of us, together," breathed Feeling, "for our path is the same." Hans felt an odorless warmth pulsing off of Feeling, but it was not the warmth of healthy life. After all, decomposing meat also generates heat.

"Gentlemen," crowed Feeling, gathering the two in an embrace, "I am a believer in process. Enlightened process. We of the Grand Malady cannot hope for instant cure. We cannot hope for perfection on the moment. We must trust to the long process, the heartfelt process, the process of grieving as it comes to us in little manageable packages. My dear Ricky, you know, my God, the message inspires me. I am inflated by its heavenly breath. I feel I must kiss your lips. Cousins? May I? You won't think it brazen, forward, intrusive or ugly for me to warm you a bit with this enthusiasm? I tell you, there, ah, thank you, dear, dear Ricky, dear friend, I shall not forget you. That's a promise I mean to keep. 'Do not forget your friend Ricky.' I'll write it down straight away. But cousins, my goodness, this life, it fills me up and I hardly know what for! I tell you, I'm brimming with the stuff! In-tu-i-tion. This is not by any means the Mayor's tepid stuff. Do you see the difference? Think of him. Think of the enormity of the man. The size of those shoes! He's comical, gentle-men, comical. And, if you will allow me a moment of seriousness, the sparkling midnight of critique, don't you think he is wrong? Just wrong? For I do believe that the Mayor imagines that the program here at our blessed Elixir will in and of itself do all the healing, suture the wounds. Oh, to hear him tell it, it's all just one vast Flask Meditation, one afternoon fellowship in the Hut, one more busy city council meeting, just keep coming, work it, 'cause it works if you work it, even slyly if you like, it doesn't matter what you think, you can think they're all morons, it doesn't matter, just strap yourself in and hold on. Am I wrong in this account of the Mayor's clinical method? Dumbly pent ritual. Routine. Repetition. But just look at it, this is the health of a robot, correct? If I thought otherwise, believe me, I'd be down there now, shoulder to the grindstone, brain pan peeled back for Hiz Honor, my dreams rising up, gathering like mist and condensing on the Mayor's bifocals. But I cannot help it, I do not believe in this method. It is stupid stuff. For I find myself always wondering, what about the Light? What about the Light, my young friends, the Holy Light? That's what heals. Breathing in the Light. It cauterizes those hurt parts of the brain. Like when you enter a room with many windows, and the warm sun pours through, scalding the world and piling high the dust motes, boiling them into the air as you approach that slash of pure light cutting the room on a diagonal and then you INHALE, friends, and you can just feel the hot dust carried on the very light, my friends, SCOURING the lungs, SCOURING the macrofila like steel wool going at a crusty pan!"

He turned Hans's shoulders so that they were nose-to-nose. "I tell you in all confidence, young Hans Castorp, this place, this place of Cure, it can kill you. It is a dangerous place. There are more dead people here than alive. Think about it. One is well advised to wear rubber soles. You know, so the dead won't hear you as you pass by."

To all of this, Ricky smiled broadly. He was plainly pleased, if not mystically ignited, by Professor Feeling's spontaneous disquisition. Hans, though, was having one of those unhappy moments that he would often have at The Elixir. He was asking in the very middle of an upright and sensitive bone in the back of his brain: Who are these people? Where am I? What language is he speaking? Why do they want to hurt me? Where is the earth? I wish to fall through it.

A tiny tear of confusion, hurt and fear gathered in Hans's eye. His lower lip curled over his upper. He could not keep his head up. "Oh," said Feeling, "look at him. I've made him feel sad with my heated talk." He put a single cold finger under Hans's chin. Hans brushed it away. "Don't be sad, little boy. I tell you what. Let's go find your buddy, Teddy. You like Teddy. He knows how to amuse you. He'll make you laugh right out loud."

They began walking back down the path, returning to downtown, the Professor and Ricky holding Hans by his hands. With each step

Hans sunk a little deeper into the earth. Within ten paces, he was up to his hips. Another ten and it looked as if they were simply dragging two detached arms in the dirt.

20

Hans could not have understood at that point in his recovery, but he had met, in Professor Feeling, a man whose personal charms were seductive, baffling and powerful. Hans often found himself with the children when the Professor told his Life Stories. He loomed above the children like a mountain. But no one seemed to think he was out of place. He was doing what came next. It was right for him to be sitting, legs crossed, with the children, listening to the Great Tales.

In this way, many of the qualities of The Elixir which were first disturbing became more familiar. That is, these people were coming to seem like family. Stranger still, Hans had begun to participate in therapies for illnesses that so far as he knew he did not have. For example, he had begun taking part in the so-called Flask Meditation. This meditation involved simply taking a flask with a brilliant scarlet E and filling it with vodka from The Fount (an enormous plastic reservoir on the back of a flatbed truck of the kind that was used in some municipalities for water emergencies), and then retreating with all the dignity and seriousness of an acolyte to one's private chambers where—door firmly bolted, blinds drawn and TV turned to re-runs of *Hawaii Five-O*—one meditated on the flask.

Actually, Hans was such a "baby," as they called him, that he really hadn't figured out (or hadn't figured out some nine days into his visit) that "meditating on the flask" in fact meant drinking it down in splendid, salubrious gulps. As they said, "Where there is great gulping, where there is the draining of draughts, can a nice, warm, numb feeling be far behind?"

21

Hans and Cecile found, through a mutual seeking that was not without purpose, a private place tucked into a sort of miniature valley created by the leaning-together of three slag heaps. A toxic grotto, you might call it. A heavy-metal bower of bliss. They would go there so that they could sit alone next to, if not exactly under, the diminutive stateliness of a stand of bonsai oak.

Theirs was an incipient *affaire de coeur* in the oldest and oddest sense. They had done nothing to this point because Hans knew how to do nothing. Even when he tried to imagine doing "something" with Cecile he could not because he was sure she did nothing (she being in his mind generally in the same place where he kept his ideas about mothers). Nonetheless, in that regard, it can't be said that the idea of mothers and "something," especially when that something had to do with blouses, cleavages and breasts, had no lure for him. In his intrigue with Cecile's blouse and the gifts it might canopy, he was in fact quite "interested" in "something." In short, he wanted to suck her breasts, latch onto them with his lips like a vivid mollusk. What came after that, he couldn't say.

At any rate, they often walked to this spot and talked and breathed.

Hans was frankly glad to be rid of the Teddies and Timmies, certainly the Professor Feelings, and, yes, even the Rickies of that world. (Although Hans did wonder what it meant that Ricky was willing to let him out of sight only when the good Frau X was in charge. Was there not something manipulative in this freedom?)

One day Hans confessed to her that he was having troubling dreams in his room at the Mr. Donut. This was an interesting confession in itself because the Mayor had been begging Hans to share just one little scrap of tattered dream with him, from which tatter he could surely fashion a sail to blow Hans who knew where. Or just one smear of dream residue, he pleaded, to culture in his mayoral Petri dish. But Hans always emphatically denied that he dreamt or that he had *ever* dreamt. To which the Mayor would reply, "Well, that's not right! A boy's got to dream! It ain't healthy! Now come on!" But Hans would no more share a dream with Mayor Jesse than he would slide his pinky finger between the Mayor's molars.

"So," the Mayor would bellow in black humor and indignation, "you're one of those no-dream-um boys, are you? Nothing but the pitted, black surface of a rock before the mind's sleeping eye? That it? Nothing but a hazy blizzard of little noiseless dots? Is that your brain? A limestone wall, is that the idea? Well, bully, bully for the boy who has no dreams!" And he'd stomp away, worried Ricky in his wake hoping to mitigate Hans's repeated and grievous *faux pas*.

Hans could just hear them. "Ricky, now you know that boy's dreamin'. Got to be. He's in the donut house, for goodness sake. Why you think we put him there? I'd be s'prised if he's not pickin' up everybody's dreams wobblin' over there on the warp and the woof. That place is like livin' in a satellite dish."

"Keep it down a little, Mr. Mayor."

"Oh, I know, but it just makes me so mad. I mean, what's my job here? What's my job?"

"I know your job, Jesse."

"Well, then, when a boy like that, with no respect, no respect at all, comes in and . . . oh, I better just go away, 'cause this has surely got me goin'."

And then Ricky's peerless look back toward Hans: "I warned you about this."

So when Hans acknowledged to Cecile that in fact the dreams were bubbling up out of him as if he slept in a cauldron, she understood the seriousness (and the trust) implicit in his gesture. "You can tell me your dreams, Hans. You can trust me." She was reaching out toward him, in a sense. It was almost as if they touched.

"Okay, but this one is a doozy. I don't really even see how it's possible that it's mine. Is it possible that I am dreaming other people's dreams? Because last night I dreamt that I was a little girl. One night my parents returned from bowling and they were very drunk. They brought a friend home with them and he was drunk too. He wore a shirt on the back of which was embroidered in bright blue letters arching over the shoulders—THE END OF HISTORY: AN AFTER-HOURS PLACE. On the front, just over his left pocket, just over his heart, it said MR. SELF.

"Mr. Self was told that he could sleep on the couch because he was too drunk to drive home. Well, in the middle of the night Mr. Self woke me up. He was whispering to me, sitting on the side of my bed. 'The sun is a very fancy fellow,' he declared. He touched my thigh. 'And we are a nation of strangers.' He sighed. 'It's a sad thing.' He pulled my legs apart. 'The spiritual possibility of finding salvation in repose has been disseminated pretty generally all over the world.' And these words struck terror into me. I tried to get away from him but discovered that my body had been turned to wood. I was really just a puppet, not a real little girl. I tried to call for help but a small brown mouse had crawled down my throat."

"Oh, Jesse would love this stuff, Hans. The things that man can do with a small brown mouse. This is beyond dream residue. You have produced high-viscosity dream glop."

"Anyway, Mr. Self said, 'It's never too late to have a happy childhood.' He spit on his hand. He said he wanted to teach me to drive a car. He was sure it could be done in one night. Suddenly, I became a bird. I was a dirty, scruffy, little sparrow."

"Now a sparrow! Jesse is expert in the interpretation of small, hand-sized animals in dreams. He's internationally known."

"I flew up. I stayed out of his reach by flapping my wings. He jumped at me with his teeth and made toothy, chawing sounds! He seemed to say, 'A-cha-cha-cha.'"

"That's when I woke up. Because I could see his teeth and my little wings were getting tired. And I was going to come down in his mouth. But when I woke up, I realized I was not alone in bed. Someone was with me. His back was to me. I grabbed his shoulder and tried to turn him toward me, certain it would be Mr. Self. But it was Professor Feeling. He pushed me away and told me to go back to sleep.

"I laid back down and closed my eyes, and said, 'Okay, this time really wake up,' and as soon as my eyes were closed they were opened and I sat up in bed and looked over for Professor Feeling, but I was all alone just like I thought. I was so confused about waking and not waking that even now I don't know if I should call this experience a dream. Perhaps it was more real than I imagine."

Cecile smiled one of those grown-up smiles mixing amusement, compassion and loads of superior knowledge. "Hans," she said, "you know, it's remarkable. I've never heard you mention your parents. Usually, the babies get here and the first thing they do is babble about mommy and daddy."

"Well, I don't think there's anything strange about it."

"Don't you want to talk about how much they hurt you and blah-blah? Not you? You're different? A different kind of boy, like Jesse says? I have to admit," and she looked oh so coquettish, "it does make you interesting. Ask the Mayor if it doesn't. But now you have at last mentioned them even if only in passing. So, they were bowlers?"

"Oh no," contested Hans, genuinely alarmed, "I have done no such thing. This was just a dream. And, like I said, I don't think it was technically *my* dream. I've never bowled. And in the dream I was a little girl but as you can see I am not a little girl. The parents must have been hers. I think her parents were on a—does this make sense?—Wednesday night Industrial League bowling team."

Hans concluded forcefully, glaring at Cecile, daring her to contradict him, "To the best of my knowledge, I can't be said to have a proper father or mother. I'm just one of those people who doesn't have parents."

"Do you take after your mother in this regard?"

"What?"

"A joke. A tiny joke."

"I don't get the humor of it."

"But really, what kind of circumlocution is this, anyway? 'Can't be said to have one.' Is that how they teach you to talk down there?"

"Cicum-what?"

"Do you mean that you don't know your parents? That you've never met them? That you're some kind of orphan?"

"Nothing so vulgar as that."

"Vulgar? What on earth . . . you think that being an orphan is vulgar?"

Suddenly, Hans became very agitated. He felt as if something he had long taken for granted were being removed. "No I don't mean anything like any of the things you think that I might be thinking. And I don't think that there is anything obscure about what I'm saying. I am simply one of those people who come about without the aid of parents."

Cecile had to laugh. "Oh where is Jesse when we need him? Do you really believe that such people exist?"

Now Hans stood and began screaming at her, furious with her levity. "No, I'm talking to you very plainly. I do not have or know anything about ever having parents. What's wrong with you? Can't you understand people when they talk?"

22

And what has Hans learned to this point? To this point, one would have to say that his moving forward is not unlike Dante's moving up toward paradise by descending down into progressively darker circles of hell. We can also say this, though: his earlier life at Downstate is now enormously irrelevant. Ask him about "group conflict resolution in an industrial setting." He'll claim never to have heard of it. Now ask him about the bloody handprint on Teddy's back. By God, he is a genius of that misery. He can read the future in the whorls of the fingerprints. That thumbprint, for example, is a terrifying journey into the beyond. He wanders in its swirling patterns. He finds it immeasurable. It invokes in him a shallow astonishment. He recalls that, in another life, he wandered from one star to another. And now he knows that that life was simply preparation for this journey into a bloody handprint on the white cotton T-shirt of a small boy. He surrenders to this shallow astonishment. Beneath his astonishment is a deeper sense of futility. Did he need to be made of the stuff of stars, imprinted with the enormous sense of design, in order to understand the meaning of the bloody handprint? Did this make sense to someone? Somewhere? He sees as a wearisome repetition all earlier limits, all the perpetual rising and passing away of experiences one after the other.

In short, Hans no longer sees things. He only sees things in things. And now, he sees his cousin Ricky's face in the handprint on Teddy's back. Ricky is smiling.

23

Because he couldn't seem to figure it out on his own, Teddy was one day obliged to show Hans the correct way to perform Flask Meditation.

"Hey, Mr. Liberal-Phoney-Baloney, you're not very observant, are you?"

"What do you mean?"

"You miss things."

"What kind of things?"

"Two at least I could name for you right now."

"Like what?"

"Like have you noticed that the light on your answering machine is blinking like it's having an epileptic seizure?"

"No. I didn't even know I had an answering machine."

"Brother. That's what I mean. Well, now you know."

"Okay, so now I know."

"Well, don't you know who that is?"

"No, I don't."

"Who do you think? Does the name LaCrema Pui Desconsolo ring a bell? She's been trying to get hold of your skinny ass for days."

"Good lord."

"Man, that bitch is gonna be hoppin' when she gets you on the line. Those Caring Caravan girls can be nasty. If I were you and I wasn't answering her calls, I wouldn't bother answering the door either. I know LaCrema. She could just plain snort a guy like you."

"How do you know this?"

"Hard and bitter experience, buddy. Hard and bitter experience. But on to another matter. What exactly do you do in here when everybody's in their room for Flask Meditation?"

"Well, I sit in here and I meditate."

"What do you mean?"

"I mean what I say. What do you mean?"

"I mean that we've noticed some things. Or not noticed some things. So tell me exactly how you do it."

"Well, what else? I think about things."

"Things? Thinking?"

"Right. Meditation. You know."

"Oh my goodness! That's all?"

"What else?"

"What kinds of things are you thinking about?"

"Oh, my experiences here, for example. Like I met Professor Feeling, and so I think about the things he said."

"You met Professor Feeling? Oh my God!"

"Is that wrong?"

"What have they got in mind for you?"

"In mind for me? How should I know? What are you suggesting?"

"In mind. *In mind*. It's okay for *them* to have something in mind. Don't you worry about that. They've always got something in mind.

Those guys are busy thinking even when we're sleeping. But, you stupid, don't you see? *You're* not supposed to have stuff in mind? You're not supposed to meet Professor Feeling and then *think* about him. That's the point of Flask Meditation. Let the Flask do your thinking."

"I don't understand."

"Oh man you are so stupid. You are so incredibly stupid. And Mister Ricky thinks I'm stupid. You're stupider. Man, what are they going to do with you? Sky's the limit, I bet. The last guy that they gave this sort of treatment to ended up spread across the sky. He was like the Big Dipper or something."

"Teddy, please be clearer."

"Okay. I'll be clearer. You're not doing what you're supposed to do, stupid."

"Like what?"

"Like you are supposed to drink what's in the flask."

"But that's alcohol."

"No shit, you dumb cuff. Fucking dumb cuff."

"I don't drink alcohol and neither should my cousin. It has a funny effect on me."

"Ha! Ha ha! You moron! It's supposed to have a funny effect on you. It has a funny effect on everyone. You are so unbelievably stupid. The milk crate I sit my butt on is smarter than you."

"But other people seem so happy when they drink. They talk more and laugh more and seem relaxed and at ease. Me, it makes me sad. I can taste my sadness as I swallow."

"God! Of course! I can't believe you! That doesn't mean you don't drink it! It means you need to drink *more*. You're going to get in a lot of trouble if they find out that you're just thinking about things.

"But maybe since they obviously have something special in mind for you, they already know that you don't drink the stuff in the flask. Hey, maybe that's why I'm here. You ever think of that?"

But Hans didn't get a chance to answer because Teddy ran over to the bed revealing again the bloody handprint on his back. It was starting to look as familiar as the logo of a Little League baseball team.

"Teddy, don't you have any other shirts?"

"No, shut up and pay attention."

Teddy threw open the drawer in the bedside table, retrieved the copy of *The Magic Mountain* and returned to Hans. He plucked the bottle from the book and then dropped the book on the floor where it landed heavily, nearly splitting the spine.

"Now watch how I do this." Teddy took a loud, noisy, messy swallow, vodka spilling down his front. "See? I can do it, and so can you! Here, try."

Hans took the bottle. Just the pale aroma of the stuff drove a little spike into his brain. A little pain spike. He took the world's tiniest sip.

"No, you fucking stupid! Are you a hummingbird or something? You think that is a flower or something? That's not how you do it." Teddy grabbed the bottle with both hands and shook it violently at Hans's mouth but also his face and eyes. "You are so stupid. You are so stupid. You are unbelievably so stupid." Hans was now forced to take large gargle-sized gulps or choke. This was a very frantic meditation indeed. Within the hour, the two had emptied the bottle into, on and around themselves.

"That's more like it," said Teddy.

Hans felt as if he had received a blow to the head. His tongue could not shape thoughts. He could not even change the direction of his gaze without great effort. His heart beat dully like a hammer in cloth.

Just when Hans seemed about to pass out, he said, "I want to see that owee of yours."

"My owee? The one Mr. Ricky gave me?"

"Yes. That one."

24

Hans pressed the message button on his answering machine. There were five messages.

"Hello! This is LaCrema Pui Desconsolo. I am an African-Thai-Mexican-American girl working my way through the Pontiac Academy of Beauty, and I am your personal friend provided for you by the Care-ring program, a service of Caring Caravan International, your first friend in your new neighborhood. Can I come down and provide you an authentic Afro-Thai-Latina welcome? Say nine-ish? Oh, but how will you know me? Well, I'll be the one standing in your doorway at nine, for starters. And I'll be wearing something silky. They're my PJs! 'Cause nine o'clock is mighty late. I love the way the fabric . . ."

Hans pressed the erase button, taking him to message number two.

"Hello again. This is your LaCrema. Well, you didn't call me back. And you sure weren't home at nine. I'm very disappointed. I had some problems with practice questions on my GED. And you're a college man! You could have helped me! There was a question in human biology about all the muscles and tendons that come spiraling up the inside of my . . ."

Erase.

"This is LaCrema. [weeping] I'm not kidding around. You've really hurt me. I'm just a poor Afro-Thai-Latina girl and I need your help with my homework. [gagging, snurfling] It's very hard for me and I don't know all the words! And I'm not used to being treated like this. In my ancient culture, a young girl is a treasure for a man! To be treated like a goddess! Which I am!"

Erase.

"This is LaCrema. [voice very dry and clipped] I've got a gun you know . . ."

Erase.

"[Terrifying silence of someone listening and waiting patiently.]"

25

Ricky saw him first.

"Look, there's little Teddy sitting on his milk crate. I think I know what he's doing. Shush. Be real quiet and we can hear him going at his self-parenting work."

Teddy said, "Daddy caught me kissing a boy good night. He called me a tramp and scared that boy off. I said, 'These are the aggressor's bonds, Daddy. These are the aggressor's bonds.' And he said, 'Teddy, you idiot, you talk like a computer.' And I said, 'Oh, Daddy, this is a terrible trap.' And he said, 'Wait a minute, Son. What is that thing? I've seen those before. I used to have one. Just like that one. Where did you get it? Huh? If mine is missing from my dresser drawer, I'm going to whale the daylight out of you. I'm going to tar the dickens out of you. Give it to me. It's no toy, Son, and that's no way to use it. Not in those tiny hands. I'll return it to you when you're old enough. In the meantime, it will just get you in all kinds of trouble.' So I said, 'Wait here, Daddy, and I'll take care of it.' And I ran in the house, past Mommy—'My, aren't we in a hurry'—and into the bathroom. I locked the door. And I said, 'Okay now take off your pants' and I took off my pants. Then I said, 'Okay now get on your knees' and

I got on my knees. 'Okay now get busy and do it right for once in your life,' and I got right down to doing it right. That was when my behavior was shrouded in misconceptions and myth. But now at last the truth can be told: I am a dirty, disgusting person."

Hans and Ricky retreated back around the corner. Hans was disturbed and confused. "Ricky," he said, "there's something going on there."

Ricky gave him one of those dead-in-the-eye looks of amazement. "Something going on? Just something? Oh shit, yes, there's something going on. Something plus something.

"You know, Hans, you think it's important to know what is serious. Oh, we see you, that look of yours, half panic, half determined apprehension. Don't think a few of us haven't been offended to our toes. Don't think your behavior hasn't been the subject of a few of the Reverend's discourses. Don't think a few of our residents haven't had to ask the Mayor for help simply because of the way you look at things and people here. It plunges a few of our more fragile sorts directly back into crisis. But it is just as important, old boy, to know what is not serious. Teddy is working through issues using self-parenting techniques he has learned here. Perhaps his conclusions at this point are enlightened and perceptive, perhaps they are preliminary. It may even be that for the time being he is on a false path. Who knows? Who cares? Everything is in process here, everything moves. Your way of looking just makes it more difficult for states of being to be. Do you understand?"

Hans was horrified. He was near tears. "No. I don't understand at all. I don't understand what you are trying to tell me. I can't help it if I have reactions to the things that happen here."

"Well try this, Cousin, rather than getting off on whatever the boys around here have stamped in blood on their T-shirts, rather than watching in that lurid way of yours, rather than having reactions to the things that happen, why not try happening yourself?"

"I see. I think I see. Be more like the others here. Be more like Teddy?"

"Exactly, old boy." So saying, Ricky laughed loudly then went around the corner walking toward Teddy, his voice full, his arms spread with the promise of a full fatherly embrace.

26

Hans's reluctance to participate, his desire to maintain a distance between himself and the residents at The Elixir was typified by his constant questioning. He once sat down with the Mayor for what was essentially an interview. It was this sort of distancing that offended Ricky and so many other Elixir residents.

Q—Thank you very much, Mr. Mayor, for agreeing to answer a few . . .

Mayor Jesse—Pesky questions!? Just a second, son. Hey, Hal, whattaya . . . Ha ha! Hal, you fuckhead! Just put it where it belongs. Ha ha! Yeah, you heard me right, fuckhead is what I said, fuckhead is what I meant. Whattaya mean what's it mean? You never heard that expression before? It means you got fuck in your head. You don't know what fuck is? Well, if that don't beat . . . Never even seen pictures, Hal? Get out of town! I'll explain it to you later. I'm busy now. Go ahead, son.

Q—Well, as I was . . .

MJ—Whoa! I don't believe that! I don't believe what I just saw, what I believe that fuckhead is up to back there. I'm real sorry about this, son. Just one more moment and you've got my undivided attention. Hey! Hal! Ha ha! Jeez. Are you a pervert or what, Hal? Well that's some of the same kind of shit we might expect from a pervert. Unbelievable. No, don't show me again, I saw it the first time. A course, I know what kind of nonsense you're up to. It's nonsense. And now the whole town knows. Good God, son, can you believe he's a growed man?

Q—He's very spirited and unpredictable.

MJ—Unpre—! Oh you don't know the half of it. He's one spirited fuckhead, he is. You don't see fuckheads that pure much anymore. He's no garden variety. Or if he is, he's like a Brussels sprout fuckhead with all those little fucked-up type Brussels heads or whatcha call 'em growin' up and down his neck.

Q—Yes. I take your meaning. But what I'd like . . .

MJ—Now wait a minute. What do you mean, "I take your meanin'"? What's somethin' like that mean? Is that some kind of special interview type talk? I said I'd talk with you, but you didn't say nothin' about talkin' like some damned computer. You're not one of those computer-talkin'-type boys, are you? "I take your meanin'." Where you gonna take it? I'll let it pass, but it's fortunate for you that I'm an understandin' fella. Cuz if it were my man Hal there, why, he's just the sort of fuckhead make a boy like you sorry.

Q—I am sorry . . .

MJ—Oh hell I don't wanna hear about how sorry you are. Forget it. Here, you want some of this before we get started?

Q—No thanks. I've had enough coffee this morning.

MJ—Coffee! Hell, son, this ain't coffee. Everythin' what's in a thermos ain't coffee. Hell no. This is Kankakee Rye Whiskey, man.

Best sippin' whiskey or gulpin' whiskey or just plain drinkin' whiskey here in Central Illinois.

Q—No thanks. I've got my own little flask now.

MJ—Well good for you! I'm glad to hear it. But after awhile those little flasks just don't cut it. They just get in the way. Try puttin' two or three of those in a coat pocket. Not just that they don't hold enough, cuz there's always more at the Fountain, but they just don't pour fast enough. A man gets frustrated. I mean I got Brussels sprout type fuckheads like Hal here around me all day, so when I need to take a belt I need to take a belt. This whatchacall interview will go a whole lot better if I keep my motor runnin'. That way, you get the "amplified affect" as opposed to the "sober interactional state" like the Professor says.

Q—Okay, can I ask my first question?

MJ—Sure, son. Go ahead. Shoot.

Q—Well, I guess I'd like to know what you think about the controversies, both recent and remote, over the therapeutic function of The Elixir and its role in state health care.

MJ—That's some question, son. Where'd you learn to ask a question like that? And I didn't even hear no question mark in it. That must be one of those clever tricks you learned at Downstate. But I think I know what you're gettin' at. You want to know how we maintain our reputation as Central Illinois' best state-supported rehab/detox facility? That's what the rest of them pussies from the newspapers want to know, too. Well, I'll tell you. I never told no one else before, but I'll tell you. I don't want no one else to hear, so bend on over this way a little . . . IT'S BECAUSE THOSE STATE SOCIAL SERVICE GIRLS ARE A BUNCH OF WEAK SISTER

BRUSSELS SPROUT-NECK FUCKHEAD PUSSIES . . .

And that's the reason why.

Q—I see.

MJ—Sure! It's because the State of Illinois is afraid of us is what it is. Sure, they got questions about our methods. Everyone does. We're famous! But they know that if they pulled our funding, which I have more than politely asked them to do, we'd be on our own. Then they couldn't touch us. We have no shortage of our own resources, man. "Funding" us gives them a little bit of contact with us, if not influence. Sure as hell ain't control. So now what we do, they give us money and we take the check up to Chicago and buy somethin' big, an abandoned building or somethin' that size, take it out to the field by the train depot and torch it. Some anthropo, anthropo-somethin' guy said this big fire made out of a gift had primitive resonance. Coffee clutch or, . . . Hal? what that Brussels sprout-neck anthropo-somethin' guy call our big fires? You don't recall? Wasn't coffee clutch, was it? Yeah, it was? What I thought. But shit that don't make no sense. Why'd a guy call a big ass fire a coffee clutch beats the hell out of me.

Anyway, that's what we do with the State's pocket change.

But they know the real deal. We got eight or nine thousand some residents out here, all of 'em good white people with money in their savings accounts and willin' to spend it for the privilege of a prolonged stay here, and we got eight buildings plus underground facilities. We pay zero taxes, have zero unemployment, zero employment and no crime. We have annexed communities around us and attract more industry and satellite corporate endeavors than all but the top ten states in the union. Our bond ratings are AAA+. Moody accountants grovel at my damn boots. You know that Mitsubishi wood chip factory over Coal City way? That's our tax base, and boy do they pay it. Seems no one else wanted the bad publicity. But shit, they were gonna grind up all those logs somewhere. Right? Ancient forests my ass.

We got every high-tech piece of bric-a-brac you can stack. ComEd runs a nuclear reactor just for us. We even have a fuckin' radar if you can believe that. Not even I know what the hell it does, but you can see the son of a bitch spinnin' round top one of the slag heaps. Recovery is like a natural resource for us. We own, I mean *own*, half the state legislature, and they are not cheap. We have a long-ass waitin' list to get in here. I have personally refused admittance to former United States presidents simply because I didn't think they'd fit in and, to be quite frank with you, I don't like their type.

But the bottom line is our clinicians have nailed their pansy asses to the hardwood on this one. We have showed in studies what the Bureau of Alcohol Research boys in Tuscola are still peein' their pants about: alcohol don't hurt nothin'! It *helps* families, man. It is part of the Ritual of Family Life and has been for some time. Without alcohol, I don't expect you could even recognize an American family. It is now a hallowed tradition. It helps grease decision makin'. Danged if it don't. It provides unique options for problem solvin'. Everyone knows this, but no one says it 'cept a few brave souls like the Reverend Boyle. Ask him, he'll tell you the truth. He knows all the facts. Hal, run get some of the Reverend's facts for the boy.

Facts aside, I can quote you chapter and verse. Take the case of Joe and Sally. Sally was a computer analyst, and Joe he just drank a whole lot. Now they had a very stable marital relationship for over fifteen years until someone made the mistake of suggestin' that Joe's drinkin' was some kind of problem. I don't remember just how they put it. So Joe cleaned up and he and Sally went into therapy. Fuckin' disaster! Joe was depressed all the time now. He'd look at ol' Sally sittin' opposite him and say, "Man alive, she's fat as sin. I am married to a fat woman. She is no foolin' a real haystack." Which I think even a bleedin' heart sensitive soul like you will admit did her no damned good. Then, of course, she'd go into the old "tearful affect." Man, a fat woman, with them big red cheeks like someone rubbed them with sandpaper, who does the old "tearful affect" is way worse than ugly. That's the sort of thing that can put you off your feed. She gives ugly a bad name.

Anyway, so Joe he's sittin' there sayin' nuthin' to nobody for weeks on end thinkin' with way more clarity than he likes, "So this is my life. Nothin' pretty about this," and old Sally just sits there like this blubber-monster of boo-hoo. I ask you, where is this cure at? You call this "better" than somethin' else?

Anyhow, we finally got old Joe and Sally up here at The Elixir and first thing we do, we put 'em in Group. And I mean this group was the group to beat all groups. We musta had two-hundred-fifty people in the old Quonset hut. Imagine two-hundred-fifty people with active substance problems in one big room. When that happens we call it Wormstock. One big nation under the Worm. And nearly as peaceful. Couldn't have been more than two or three fistfights on the periphery. Everybody'd heard about this big fat composition of a computer woman who goes boo-hoo and her skinny salesman drunk of a husband. Just the thought was pornographic. So you know we sit 'em down, get three or four foldin' chairs propped around old

Sally and first thing I say is, "Joe, you know, why don't you have a little taste before we get started?" And he looks at me wide-eyed, as if I was tryin' to trick him. So I say, "Joe, lookit, we're gonna get you where you wanna go. But we got irregular means. We're not like all the rest. We're what they call unusual." And so he says, "Well, how about that? Whattaya got?" And I say, "We got Kankakee Rye is what we got." So I hand him this very thermos right here and he pours himself a nice transfusion. Well, wasn't long before old Joe jumps up out of his so-called depression. A mean deprivation of basic human rights is more like what it was. A man has got to be allowed the requisite tools to face the damned day. Now he's assertive, angry and demandin' and now he wants to know why it is that old Sally never wants to have sex with him. Well now, don't you see?, we've got these difficulties in the open. Joe's got more stuff to get in the open. He's got baggage. He's got issues like everybody else. Because of old Sally, he's sure got the "when women get old they get ugly" issue or a very chubby version thereof. Some people don't like that issue and don't think of it so much as an issue as an insult, but I say, hell, open your damned eyes! And Joe's goin' on about how fat his little buttery squab of a wife has become and why the heck don't she get a NordicTrack or somethin' to take the edge off this meat mountain. Sally, she says that she has a complaint, too. She says unless old Joe's drunk he has no sexual interests at all and in fact drunk or sober has had not even a noddin' acquaintance with an erection in these last seven or eight years. Then comes the old tearful affect again. Oh boy! Group is dyin' out there. They're breakin' up. Fallin' out. Makin' like a bunch of whoopin' cranes on a funny drug. So this is the famous butterball of boo-hoo. But then, old Joe's little sneaky fingers are strokin' the inside of her dimpled thigh, and he don't seem to know where to stop. We lost sight of his hand. But she don't seem to notice one way or the other. Lookit, in my opinion, her leg o' lamb was just too damned thick for nerve endings. I mean, you get this fat just goin' on and on, deep like some peat bog, and the nerve endings I believe get lost and confused. So while she's goin' boo-hoo, he's just gropin' away, heedless.

Meanwhile, Group is lovin' this stuff. Wormstock. Fat women havin' sex, drunks with nothin' hard about 'em, and everythin' bathed in boo-hoo. I'll tell it like it is: while Joe and Sally were residents here, this place was alive. Nothin' that interestin' come this way again till a certain college boy from Downstate who shall go nameless.

But my point is, don't you see, that Joe and Sally were better able to demonstrate a wide range of behaviors, more capable and comfortable engagin' each other, more attentive to each other's feelings when we added a little Kankakee Rye to the equation. With alcohol in the picture, Joe could become flirtatious and sexual. And Sally, feelin' disgusted and degraded by his dirty drunken pawin', was able to deflect her guilt at bein' the portly cause of her husband's impotence.

What Sally and Joe achieved with our help was a clearer understandin' of what the Professor calls "the emotional economy central to their relationship" whatever the hell all that means. What I say is, sobriety! Don't make me laugh! It's just not good for everyone. You got to learn to work alcohol. It'll work if you let it. Hunnert percent promise. Last I heard, Sally was still bein' mistaken for landscapin' and Joe was still catchin' furniture on fire in his zealous housekeepin', *and* they are still married.

Some people like to talk about "let's get real." Okay, let's get real. Nobody's gonna strap Sally to a machine and jiggle off three hundred pounds. And no one's gonna get Joe's dingle to do more than flap in the wind. The Worm has its own path. It's a shiny one. Let the Worm find its path is what I say.

27

We are privileged to be able to describe for you an old family film of Hans and his cousin in some bright suburban backyard. They are maybe nine-years-old. They are playing as their fathers watch, beers in hand. The fathers are encouraging the boys to wrestle. The boys do so. The film is very unsteady, unfocused. Now a small dog runs around. A black dog with white patches. It wags its tail, no one knows quite why. (It was something that people expected of dogs in that time. A happy dog was a general reflection of family well-being.) Now Ricky is pretending to smoke his father's pipe. He laughs. In the next scene, Ricky tackles Hans. It's football and good fun. Then somehow Hans has run his head into a barbed wire fence and blood is pouring down his face. This was not part of the football game. Or perhaps it was. Hard to say. In any event, he is crying. His face is marbled with tears and blood. Cut to Ricky who is still laughing. It is a laugh of the kind that was called "savage." But he also seems older as well as savage, so perhaps he is laughing on another day altogether. It would be bestial, after all, to laugh savagely while his cousin bleeds. In fairness, perhaps he won the football game and is simply enjoying his great victory. That would explain it. Back to Hans's bloody face where strange detached hands wipe at him with Kleenex. Motherly figures turn in circles laughing silently about Hans's latest foul-up. So there is a "cute" aspect to the disaster. Kids are like that. They do the darndest things. Ramming their little heads into barbed wire, for example. The Kleenex tears into soggy wads making the boy's face look like crimson papier-mâché.

Now it is plainly a very different day, a day of gloomy overcast. Hans is pacing nervously around a large clothes hamper which for some reason is in the middle of the yard. It is the same suburban backyard. The hamper is one of those pastel wicker affairs with a plastic lid. There are daisy flowers applied to the outside, as if a hamper were really a very sunny, happy and pleasant thing. What we don't know is why the hamper is in the middle of the backyard. Is this what mothers used to call a "stunt"? Or "childish antic"? Or "prank"? Hans opens the top of the hamper and looks inside. A look of anguish is on his face. His lips pucker as if he would like to blow bubbles. He closes the lid and returns to pacing around the hamper, very agitated. Something must be in that darned hamper. Again he opens the top and peers inside. He shakes his head. It appears something is quite wrong. It would appear that there is a profundity in the hamper. The camera approaches. Hans gestures violently to the camera telling it and its operator to stay away. He waves it back. He seems to want to save the camera from certain disaster. He runs headlong, arms outstretched, at the camera, disappearing briefly beneath the lens. Suddenly a huge and distended head like something out of a funhouse mirror overwhelms the lens. A large, male arm emerges from behind the camera and knocks Hans down to the ground. Now the hamper is rocking crazily side-to-side like a cocoon. It's going to burst forth at any second. The male hand lifts the top of the hamper as if to release the great pressure there. But it's just little Ricky inside the hamper. Is he dead? Ricky looks up. He's not dead. He grins. Then he squirms in his enclosure and thrusts his hips upward revealing a soda bottle wedged into his crotch. It is a large soda bottle for such a young boy and very brilliant green in the camera light. The camera turns back to Ricky's face. He is laughing and screaming and saying things. This is what the phrase "maddened delight" describes. His mouth is moving like crazy. His teeth flicker. What is he saying? These are old words. Words little boys said a long time ago. The lid is dropped back down on the hamper. The camera backs away very slowly, careful to keep its eye on the receding hamper. A nice job by somebody. Very steady hands. A sort of German expressionist angularity is achieved. The camera remains fixed upon the hamper, waiting for Ricky to emerge. But Ricky doesn't come out. The scene goes on for a long time. Once, Ricky's head bobs out of the hamper like a jack-in-the-box and he screams, laughing. It looks like he's saying "Jell-O," but that doesn't make any sense. Over and over again. Just "Jell-O." Hans sprawls by the side of the hamper, his face buried in the crook of his arm. The camera stops and holds the hamper and bereft Hans in its gaze for a very long time. Hours pass. Days. The hamper obtrudes from the barren yard as if it were a reliquary.

28

One day, Hans was sitting with his cousin Ricky in the Daffy's, his dinner before him, grayish margarine coagulated over reconstituted mashed potatoes. He was staring at the margarine, watching it stiffen, and yet feeling vaguely that something at the molecular level of Being was beginning to oscillate dangerously. The visible world thickened, but the atomic world felt as if it might fly apart. He was wondering if he dared ask Ricky if there was any need to worry that the glue of existence might at some moment simply fail. Now the margarine and potatoes seemed to smolder as if they could burst into flames. He looked at Ricky, but Ricky's thoughts were somewhere else. Ricky's dinner was eaten to the last speck. Nothing about molecules or margarine or the glue of Being coming undone kept Ricky off his feed. And now he enjoyed a cigarette in a perfect, self-possessed, meditative calm. Thus the miracle of the flask, thought Hans. It worked so well for him. On the other hand, Hans didn't dare tell Ricky how he felt. If he did, Ricky would be disappointed at the least. Probably disgusted. He would reject Hans. Hans would be alone and abandoned. Without hope. He wouldn't even be able to think clearly enough to figure out how to use the train and leave. He imagined himself sleeping on the sidewalk curled up around Teddy's plastic milk crate.

At just that moment the cousins saw to their side the graceful movements of Cecile as she entered and searched for a table. She seemed to see Hans first and there was the beginning of a friendly smile and conspiratorial wink. But then she looked at Ricky and she became self-conscious, perhaps embarrassed, as people are when they associate someone with something shameful that they've done. Curiously, Hans found himself envying Ricky's ability to produce such responses in people, especially in Cecile. He'd seen it many more times than once. Cecile barely managed an awkward nod at the two young men and then sat down by herself at a distant table.

Ricky saw how completely Cecile had captured his cousin's attention. He laughed and put out his cigarette.

"Old boy," he said, his smoky chuckle rising up, "you'll bore a hole in her with that look."

"What?"

"You're hard-a-lee toward the obvious, Cousin."

Hans bluffed hopelessly. "What do you mean?"

"I mean Frau X, that heedless, charming creature. You're not the first to find her a happy destination for the eyes." A downy red patch on Ricky's cheek grew darker, as if healthy blushing cheeks were really live coals.

"She's no big deal. She's a sort of lumpy librarian in my opinion. And she's too old for me."

Ricky patiently lit another cigarette and exhaled a huge cloud into the air above his head. He held the little burning eye of the cigarette directly in front of his face. He peered through the haze. "Right," he said. "But you're not too young for her, and that's all that really matters around here."

"Who is she?" asked Hans. "Is she really German?"

"No. She's from San Francisco. That's exotic enough for you, I suppose. Her husband might be German."

Hans's shoulders dropped. "She's married?"

Ricky laughed conspicuously. He was enjoying Hans's visit. The babies were always good for a laugh. "Yes, she is married. Her husband visited her here once, for a weekend. God, wasn't that a debacle! I doubt that he'll be back. It's a pity because Herr X showed himself for the true Elixir type during his short stay. Oh well. I suppose we need some ambassadors. At any rate, married or not, don't let it worry you. It doesn't worry anybody else."

Hans was appalled. He slapped his hand down on the table and whispered angrily to his cousin, "That's enough. I've heard just exactly enough of that kind of awful innuendo around here. I know Cecile, and I won't listen to this hateful and demeaning talk."

Ricky giggled. For a moment he was again the little, perverse creature Hans had known as a boy. A gremlin in a hamper with a soda bottle jammed into his crotch. His downy, boyish cheeks flamed. "Hans, Hansel, Hansy, old boy, little cousin, she will take your two tiny balls between her lips and treat them as gently and sweetly as a goldfish blowing bubbles. Ask her and see if she won't." And he collapsed in jejune titters.

Hans couldn't help looking over to Cecile's table. She nodded demurely as if in assent, and then cast her eyes down, smiling quietly. Hans, for his part, was reminded that the auburn waves of her hair were perfect. Perfectly sinister.

Ricky sat bolt upright, again his severe self. When he did that suddenly you could almost hear the distant military click of heels. "Well," he said, "she's a pathetic thing in any case and she'll soon be at her last gasp. Her illness is galloping. It really won't be long. I hear that under Reverend Boyle's guidance she has begun talking to the Blue Peter. That's never a good sign."

Hans couldn't even begin to wonder what a Blue Peter was.

29

That same evening, as Hans dressed for bed, he felt agitated and breathless. He couldn't breathe comfortably even through his mouth. His clothing felt like restraining straps. Someone seemed to be hugging him so violently that he felt faint. He took off his shirt and laid it on the bed.

On the back of the shirt was the faint outline of a reddish handprint.

30

The afternoon "Group sessions" were led by the boisterous Mayor Jesse in the Quonset hut. Because Hans was still afraid to go inside the hut, these sessions remained mysterious to him. He couldn't quite figure them out. They, literally, didn't add up. Obviously, the space was large. It was something built to hold an aircraft, after all. Obviously, it could hold hundreds. And, obviously, the thunderous roars that came from inside could only be made by a large number of men. But Hans never saw more than a few small groups of men enter. He would watch the hut. At 11:30 it was quiet. Around 11:55 he might see a pair of stumbling men enter. By 12:10 the hut was barking out its anger, disgust and disappointment like a bad-tempered and hollow-chested dog. The question was, when had all these men entered? Where had they come from? We might say that if Hans really wanted to know, all he had to do was go inside and check it out. Unfortunately, it was clear to Hans that to take part in "Group" in the cavernous hut was to cross a line, was to admit to a relationship with The Elixir and its residents that he was not ready to admit to because . . . he was afraid. So he would hang around outside the hut at Group time, attracted and curious but unwilling to participate himself.

Often Ricky would watch with him. Hans was glad to have his cousin sit with him. Still, he felt a little ridiculous, as if Ricky were in some way holding his hand. Hans also wondered why Ricky wasn't inside with the others. Didn't he need counseling? Whatever the case, he was glad to have Ricky with him to help interpret the many strange things he heard.

After the first two weeks (for, yes, Hans had decided to extend his stay and had sent a fax to his new employer explaining the severity of his cousin's case and requesting an additional two-week delay in the commencement of his tenure at noble Caterpillar), the loud roars became familiar and predictable. The racial and sexual obscenities that drifted out like smoky exhalations were merely ordinary now. But the curious periods of utter quiet, spaced here and there in the proceedings, what were they about? The little periods of quiet were often followed by outbursts of hollow laughter. Hans imagined that the Mayor was telling funny stories with his fingers. But on two occasions during this period the quiet was followed by a loud bang that reverberated out of the hut in long, aching, nauseating waves. Wasn't that what a gun sounded like? Hans wasn't sure he'd ever actually heard a gun before. But wasn't that what they sounded like? The bang was followed by the profound, almost reverential silence in which human beings cloak themselves in the aftermath of the consequential and infinite play of His Majesty the Gun. Go to the ghetto of your choice and stand on a street corner. Listen for the Great Report. It doesn't matter if anyone is actually shot. The world is different after a gunshot. It's like church. It's like the world at prayer.

When Hans finally asked Ricky about the weird silences, the queer and dizzying silences, Ricky seemed genuinely surprised. It was as if for Ricky the answer were so obvious and yet so much in need of asking from the very first day that he had come to assume that Hans had figured it out on his own. Or that he would never ask. It couldn't occur to Ricky—because he was so intensely aware of everything—that Hans had simply not noticed. It could, on the other hand, occur to him that Hans was, after all, not one of his brighter students. So when he was confronted with the unmistakable fact that Hans was missing things that he shouldn't be missing, it made him a little irritable. It was like realizing that the student you were tutoring was not paying attention, was not paying any attention at all, and had not the slightest idea what he was studying. This is why, as even Hans noticed, Ricky's reaction to his question had something of the bloom of anger in it.

But the fact was that he didn't really say anything. The bloom of anger came when Ricky looked intently into Hans's eyes. Ricky simply extended his glowing index finger and touched Hans between his eyes. Then the strangest thing happened. Hans heard a very distinct "pop" that seemed to come from somewhere deep inside his own head. If he were an older man, Hans might have suspected that it was a blood vessel. But he did not suspect this because out of the popping emerged a fissure and out of the fissure came a vision, clumsily black and white, of the kind we were provided in early movies when the audience was being shown what was going on inside a character's head. In the scene that darkly emerged in Hans's brain, a man was sitting on a platform in front of a seated crowd. A bulky figure (the Mayor, no doubt) handed the man a gun. The man looked like a farmer. He was large. He was a hill-like man. He wore blue overalls. He wore a cheap green jacket. He wore a Cargill Seed cap. His hands

were like slabs. His overalls were stained at the crotch so conspicuously that Hans imagined he could smell the urine. The man smiled
self-consciously. He was a little goofy. He was like someone fated to
freeze to death outside his trailer home one drunk January evening.
There was a low tittering, like an audible sneer, in the crowd. The
Mayor handed the man a sheet of paper from which he was encour-
aged to read.

"Oh you of the rosy childish face," the man read.

"Oh you of the rosy childish face," the crowd repeated.

"Grown dense with whiskers."

"Grown dense with whiskers."

"Most of them gray."

"You're older, my friend."

"Know that the revolver is a piquant tool."

"A learning tool!"

"And it is a shiny thing."

"You've kept it clean!"

"And know that when we place it to our skull . . ."

"When you place it very carefully to your skull."

"Do we not hear the sea inside?"

"Inside our skulls?"

"Yes. And does it not surge like surf?"

"The whole ocean is in your little head."

"But it is not surf, it is the surging of the very blood in our
heads."

"The blood in your skull is a great tempest."

"It is then we ask the ponderous question . . . Is life precious?"

"Precious you say?"

"Precious."

"And?"

"And we reply . . ."

"Reply."

"Where there is the agreeable sensation of being totally lost and abandoned."

"Where we are abandoned."

"Where we can say, 'I don't count here; I need do nothing more; and laugh at the whole thing.'"

"The whole thing is damned funny."

"And where shame has certain clear advantages over honor."

"Hallowed be thy shame, my friend."

"Then is a man relieved of the burden of a respectable life and may shudder in a wild wave of sweetness."

"Sweet! Sweet!"

The farmer then rose, holding the paper with his ritual verses before him.

"And say, seven come eleven, see if that dulcet worm don't tickle my brain."

The farmer then stuck the barrel of the revolver to the side of his head. Hans screamed, covering his face with his hands. After a moment, he looked up again at Ricky, gasping, wondering if his cousin had really caused this snapping of vessels and this flood of images.

Ricky wasn't letting on. He appeared perturbed and disgusted. He said, "Look, Cousin, I can't babysit for you out here forever. Those are my people in there. No one is making you stay. If you need to get on a train, we've got tractors that will take you there. So, if you don't like it here, get the fuck out."

At just that moment, Hans noticed that the stinking air was back. It smelled as if somewhere not far off household appliances were piled to the sky and burning in a great bonfire. He looked distracted.

Ricky muttered in disgust . . . "fucking moron" . . . and stared at Hans. "What's the matter with your brain? Have you been napping out by the Atrazine landfill?" Hans said nothing. "Good lord," concluded Ricky, turning away, leaving Hans alone with The Elixir's smoky, smelly exhalations purling around him.

31

If Hans woke at 3:00 A.M., as he now routinely did, he would hear a voice whispering to him. Where did this voice come from? It was the voice of Mr. Donut. It was the concentrated voice of all the little pastry people who had eaten there and in eating there had confessed their nullity. It would repeat its frightened thought as if it were a metronome and each little thought were a way of measuring time. It repeated its thought two-thousand-and-twelve times. Its thought went like this:

"Something terrible is going to happen to you.

"It is the only certainty in your life.

"It's waiting out there for you.

"A beast.

"Many terrible things are going to happen to you.

"This is a personal failure.

"You have no one to blame but yourself."

Hans could feel pain waiting for him like heat from an open furnace at the end of a very long hall.

Then the voice began its little recitation again, "Something terrible is going to happen to you."

Mr. Donut never went to sleep. He wanted to stay up all night and party. Hans? Hans Castorp? Wake up, I want to play! Mr. Donut turned on the TV. Mr. Donut moved things around on the counter. He ground coffee for the morning. He scurried in the bedside table drawer like a tiny mouse. He nibbled on Hans's fingers and toes.

"Hansel! Hansy!"

"What!?"

"Something terrible is going to happen to you."

The phone rings. Who can be calling at 3:00 A.M.?

In a daze, Hans answers. Is it Mr. Donut calling him up? Is there no limit to his evil? Infect his sleep then wake him to show that his waking is just as corrupt?

"Oh, so you do answer your phone sometimes, you fucking little twerp. This is LaCrema. I am a beautiful woman with a proud ethnic character, asshole, and I don't need to be jerked around by a little nothing scum bag like you. If you know the meaning of those big words, Mr. College Man! I got guys hangin' on the phone all over Pontiac and the greater Mid-state Downtown Nexus. So you stay right there. You owe me and I'm comin' to collect."

32

What Hans could never possibly understand is the idea that everyone around him understood him in a way that he could never understand himself. This is self-knowledge twice removed. Even the Mr. Donut building seemed to understand Hans better than he understood himself. Hans had the habit of thinking of his feelings as unique, individual. This was of course an error, a fundamental error. But others, especially the aptly-monikered Professor Feeling, saw Hans as merely typical. He was predictable, maybe even trite. Thus the odd mixture of sympathy/understanding and ennui/impatience Hans inspired in those more-knowing others around him.

Professor Feeling was in fact an expert in the Alcoholic Family System out of which Hans had emerged. Professor Feeling was himself the so-called "clinical variable" in a series of highly controversial studies funded by The Elixir. The studies involved visiting the homes of alcoholic families during the evening hours of one especially gloomy September. The research team was interested in family rituals in alcoholic families. Video tapes were made, the best of which were distilled by The Elixir's Entertainment Committee into a single ninety-minute diversion for those days on which The Elixir hadn't the energy to create its own diversions (let it be known, those days were few and far between).

A written description and analysis was also made, from which I quote:

Alcoholism and Family Ritual
By Mr. Self, M.C.

The importance and power of rituals in primitive societies or in religious groups is well known. Rituals reinforce the shared beliefs and common heritage of those who take part in them. With their prescribed form and unchanging content, rituals help those who perform them make sense of their particular social universe. Contrary to the common perception that ritual is of no account or is even entirely missing in the chaotic environment of the alcoholic household, we have found that alcoholic families in fact do have very well-defined rituals which they respect with a fervor no less intense than that fervor which prevails in non-alcoholic families.

We divide the types of ritual here studied into two dominant categories: the everyday or Quotidian Ritual and the 'Special' or Epiphanic Ritual.

For example, let us consider Subject Family 421.

[This was, in fact, as was well known within the amused community of The Elixir, the Castorp family. The original referral to the Castorp family was provided by cousin Ricky's mother, who had herself participated in an earlier study called, "Alcoholic Wives and Immodesty: A Cross-referential, Diachronic, and Reverse-regressive Study of the Stability of Moral Signifiers: Drunkenness, Libidinal

Profligacy and Indecent Exposure." (Excerpts from the very same study were available on DVD and VHS as "Snatch Time: Drunk Wives Gone Wild" if you visited the right website.) The study referred to those moments when an alcoholic woman's intoxication crossed that always mobile line which allowed her to sufficiently lose touch with her culturally conditioned "modesty" (a term that the staff struggled mightily with, suspecting that it had little if any power to mean anything in this context) so that publicly exposing her breasts or genitals became, as it was said, "no problem." The study's particular focus on "alcoholic wives" rather than "women" was a reflection of the fact that in a good many instances the wives in the study were the wives of residents at The Elixir, which fact added a certain "aggregate" to the findings. The term "aggregate" itself is worthy of comment. The men of The Elixir (a cross-section of Central Illinois's men and so on the whole a rough bunch) imported the term from the system for grading the coarseness of sandpaper. So, if one were to say, "That's a forty grit on Tom's nose," for example, this was a very humiliating and painful experience on the "aggregate" measuring rubric. Thus, the resourceful thinking of the study design team allowed them to measure not only the extremity of the drunken wife's conduct during indecent exposure but the appropriate degree of humiliation for the husband (course, medium, and fine or 40, 80 and 120 for the aficionado) as measured on the "aggregate" scale. It is significant to note that The Elixir would hardly have been interested in the issue of, as Mayor Jesse put it, "drunk women airing their privates," if it hadn't opened up avenues for investigation among the male residents of The Elixir (historically 80% of the population). It was in fact a "coarse" interpretation of one Ricky Castorp's mother's conduct with a group of Catholic high-school boys in the back of a pickup camper that led, eventually, to his own plan of treatment at The Elixir. Bluntly, Ricky had joined a line of boys from St. Ignatius in which a "train" was being "pulled" by a drunken woman. When it was Ricky's turn, he heard laughter and whispering outside. What he didn't hear or understand until too late was the reason for the laughter: "Oh my God, Ricky's doing his own mom." This was 20 grit, floor sander, off-the-chart quality "ouch" on Ricky's young nose. The Castorp family on Hans's side, upon learning of this incident, had forbidden future contact between Hans and Ricky and had generally ostracized Ricky's family. It was thus with a touch of vindictiveness that she (Ricky's mom, Hans's aunt) had suggested "those nice Castorps" to the study team.]

The quality of so-called Quotidian Ritual consists of three measurable variables: location, variation and synchrony. The study team carefully mapped the Castorp home for its available spaces and entered them on a grid. The available spaces were living room, dining room, kitchen, master bedroom, second bedroom, bathroom, front porch, front yard, backyard and hamper. (Note: the team was obliged to add "hamper" because on several relevant occasions young Hans [thirteen at the time] got into the dirty clothes hamper and closed the top down on himself, in which place he stayed for hours at a time or until a particularly noxious scene could be concluded.) Then, by adding a diachronic scale along the bottom of the grid, a measurement of family movement could be gained which would range from "lethargy" to "extreme agitation." Hence for Hans Castorp's father:

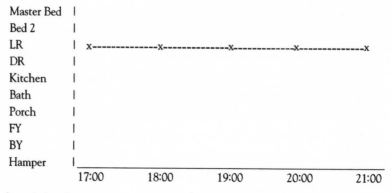

```
Master Bed |
Bed 2      |
LR         | x--------------x--------------x-------------x-------------x
DR         |
Kitchen    |
Bath       |
Porch      |
FY         |
BY         |
Hamper     |_____
            17:00        18:00        19:00        20:00        21:00
```

*= verbal exchange

However, for Hans's sister, Gretel, the graph looked like this:

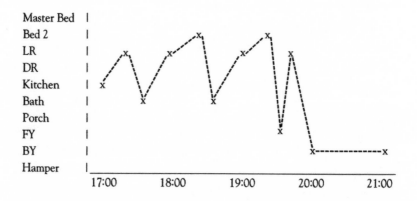

```
Master Bed |
Bed 2      |               x,          x,
LR         |      ,x    x--x  \   x--x/  \   x
DR         |     /   \ /       \ /      \ / \
Kitchen    | x  /     x         x        x   \
Bath       |  /      x           x            \
Porch      |                                   \
FY         |                              x     \
BY         |                                     x-------------x
Hamper     |_____
            17:00        18:00        19:00        20:00        21:00
```

Hans's father and sister perfectly define the extreme clinical states of "lethargy" and "agitation." (Note: some critics of this study have suggested that in fact in most of these evenings Hans's father was in fact passed out drunk and is for that reason an acceptable example of no particular pattern of "behavior." One waggish clinician went so far as to suggest that since Castorp *père* appeared never to have moved a muscle on any night of the study period that he had in fact died.) Let's take a look at young Hans's graph on a typical evening just to get another snapshot of what the "ritualized" family routine might have looked like in the Castorp family.

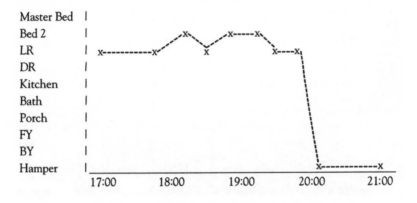

Young Hans's graph, by comparison, has a relatively healthy rhythm in its progression. It is neither lethargic nor agitated. One should note, however, that as the evening progresses a troubling pattern, not unlike his sister's, emerges in his increasingly rapid movements between the living room and his bedroom. The qualitative researcher would certainly be tempted to comment that the living room space contains a classic "mixed emotional signal" for the boy. It has, on the one hand, the calming and entertaining presence of the television set, and, on the other, the disturbing presence of the drunken father with the television remote. Thus, his mild agitation is caused by the frequent and unpredictable interruptions in the television programming caused by the troubled waking of his father who would then proceed to flip between channels without apparent reason, as if it were no more than his hand having spasms on the channel button. Since Hans had no recourse or appeal to his father's intoxicated whimsy (short of taking the radical and patricidal option of claiming the remote control device for himself), he was left, psychically, in a disconnected, always-unfinished nowhere, to which unhappy state he would respond by retreating first to his room and then, ultimately, to the dirty clothes hamper where he stayed until 23:00 hours. At that point he came out only in order to go to bed.

The larger question for measurement, diagnosis and therapy remains: is there an essential difference between the behavior of Hans and his sister? One might suggest that the only real difference is that Hans had what the research team called "pockets of retreat" from family space while his sister, Gretel, seemed for unknown reasons not able to define or identify such spaces for herself. Unless, of course, one would wish to say that her ultimate retreat to the backyard, festooned with the family dog Poochie's excrement, was a "pocket of retreat." (The research team considered and rejected this possibility.) On any descriptive scale, the simple fact that she seems to have fallen asleep out there would make categorizing it as such a "pocket" untenable.

Final note: the measurement instrument that we have employed here does in fact have a rubric (*) indicating "verbal exchange," but it is not part of this graph because, simply, so-called "verbal exchange" was not a part of the Castorp family's "Quotidian Ritual." The only exception here, as already noted, would be the father's occasional dark commentary directed, apparently, to the TV itself.

Last, of course, we provide the movements of the mother.

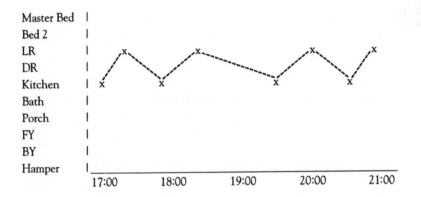

If we superimpose all of our four graphs one on the other, we have a revealing "snapshot" of the family on any given night. It is a perfect image of the alcoholic family system. Hence:

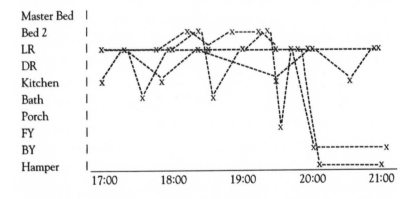

Next, we move to the Epiphanic Ritual. This is what is commonly called "Special" time in most households (i.e., Christmas and other holidays, but especially Christmas). Here, the Castorps were no different from others. The Castorp family ritual had nothing to do with elaborate preparations for Christmas stretching back for weeks and involving decorating the house, gift buying and the endless mutual congratulation of friends. Rather, the Castorp Christmas ritual consisted of one forty-five minute period on Christmas morning when the family would gather round the Christmas tree to open presents. This, obviously, is a scene repeated in millions of American homes on Christmas morning. Since, however, the Castorp household was also an alcoholic household, their Epiphanic Ritual had one decidedly unique twist. During the course of this Special morning, Father Castorp (a hungover Father Castorp on a statistical probability of 99.9%) would ignore the drinking of cocoa, the eating of rolls, and the opening of presents and insist instead on his need/right to watch a football game on the television set which loomed above the family like an ominous teetering rock. At a certain point each year, one of the family members (this richly symbolic role was passed from member to member each year) would suggest, "Dad, why don't you turn off the TV for a little while? We're opening presents." To which Dad's ritual response was invariably, "God damn it, I'm watching the God damned football game, and if you don't like it you can all go in the other room." This apparently straight-forward comment was treated, by the family, as oracular and enigmatic. There was usually no direct reaction to it. Rather, it was pondered by the rest of the family as if it were a rune. ("What do you think Dad meant?" "Why did he say that?" "Doesn't he like presents?") This is not unusual. In ritual space, the ordinary becomes the extraordinary; in ritual space, plain speech becomes enigmatic. The family members—excepting the children, to whom I will return—exchanged looks which asked, "How can we understand the expression 'go away, I'm watching TV' to mean 'Merry Christmas, I love you all, and what did Santa bring you?'?" This is the sort of riddle that gives classical mythology its life. The children, on the other hand, were not capable of such a cognitively sophisticated translation. For them, the effect of Father Castorp's pronouncement was to add heat to their already simmering psyches. Very gradually, like gently rising heat in a pan of popcorn, they began to rise and fall with increasing vehemence finally reaching a point where Mother Castorp was trying to hand Hans a present as he bounded three to five feet in the air on the family sofa. To which Father Castorp's response was, following ritual formulation, "Can't you keep the God damn racket down?"

By these marks are families known.

In the year following the study, the original test families were re-visited by the clinical/diagnostic teams in order to test the effects of introducing into well-established ritual patterns (both quotidian and epiphanic) a so-called variable. The variable in each case was a well-trained and long-term resident of The Elixir. This variable, in the case of the Castorp family, was one Professor Feeling. Professor Feeling's peculiar (one wants almost to say "alien") presence was injected into the midst of family ritual with unpredictable results all of which confirmed that all households, whether dry or alcoholic, have powerful regulating family rituals. When that ritual organization is disturbed by the introduction of a foreign element (a very apt description of Feeling's presence), nothing is as it "ought" to be. For instance, during the time of Feeling's introduction into Castorp Quotidian Ritual Reality, the following state-of-mind was described by Father Castorp:

"I can't sleep. There's something ominous and threatening in the house. It's going to get me. I have to stay awake. I believe the house is possessed."

In addition, Mr. Castorp identified the following "uncanny" events:

• the television remote was repeatedly "lost" and just as inexplicably "found";

• Hans's hamper was discovered on the curb on garbage day;

• Gretel began sleeping in her bed instead of with the dog excrement in the backyard.

All of these eventualities were described by Mr. Castorp as "spooky."

Since it has already been broadly reported in both professional and popular criticism of this study, we will acknowledge the report (if not the fact) that on at least one night Professor Feeling actually slept with Mother Castorp. (The clinical observer's reaction to this particular event was the hand-tied gnashing of clinical teeth.)

Mr. Castorp was ultimately confronted with the idea that a member of the clinical team had slept with his wife through a report that appeared on the popular program "America's Most Humiliating Home Videos." He is described as rising from his couch, tripping over the coffee table, falling, and landing heavily on his shoulder (the right). From this painful, awkward and—again—humiliating posture, he is said to have tried to invoke the ritual protocols and language of the "Wrath of Dad." Professor Feeling is said to have acted as if he were a dog rolling on the ground "laughing to see such sport."

The children, for their part, acted as if their hair were on fire.

On the morning of the epiphanic ritual—that is to say, Christmas—
Professor Feeling crouched on the floor with the family members
and enjoyed hot cocoa and sweet rolls. Being a little tightly wound
by nature, he was even a little more inspired by the sugar and cocoa
than the children were. His "variable" presence yielded predictably
"special" (or exaggerated, explosive, accelerated, and even demonic)
results. Understand, as a clinical variable it was Professor Feeling's
responsibility to introduce destabilizing or simply challenging ir-
regularities into the flow of regular ritual activity. In this way is the
strength of ritual practice tested. This variable moment occurred
when it came time for Dad to make his epic pronouncements vis-
à-vis the importance of the football game. Now, Dad was already
rather tensely aware of Professor Feeling's variable presence by this
point in the study. As we've had cause to mention, the Professor had
spent many long hours clad in the rags of Castorp family quotidian
ritual with prominent results. Thus, no sooner were the hierophantic
words "God damn it. I'm watching the God damn . . ." out of Dad's
mouth than Professor Feeling jumped to his feet, threw his long and
flamboyant scarf around his neck and shouted, "Did you say football?
I love that fucking game!" He then stood in front of the TV and,
worse yet, in front of Mr. Castorp, bouncing up and down like a
possessed puppet. When Mr. Castorp began yelling that he couldn't
see the game, Feeling said, "Are you too far away?" Then quickly
and powerfully he lifted the TV from its stand and carried it over
to Castorp the Elder and dropped it in his lap, rather heavily, thus
pinning him in "Father's chair" as if he were some wriggling bug on

a pin. For its part, the family members went quickly from shock and dismay to epic glee and back again all depending on which was more striking, Dad's curses and threats or the amusing spectacle of Dad pinned in his favorite chair beneath the TV.

The "Feeling variable" achieved considerable notoriety in clinical circles because he was the first such variable to "go autonomous." That is, the force of his variable character was so pronounced that his original variable function began to seem to all concerned murky at best. Meanwhile, the centrality of his role in the family system—challenging and usurping the alcoholic father—was crystal clear. It might be added that, from the perspective of The Elixir's concerns in the study, this was an "okay" result. The consultants, however, who had designed the study's empirical tools were very unhappy about the conduct of the variable and they were furious that it had "gone autonomous." They denied that the notion of a Variable Gone Autonomous had any scientific legitimacy. They made particular reference to a) the possible displacement of the father to the streets, b) the destruction of the family TV, and c) the utterly unacceptable possibility of a variable-gened offspring incubating in Mrs. Castorp. The consultants at last obtained a court order returning Professor Feeling to The Elixir complex at which point, with an enormous sigh of relief, the Castorp family was able to resume its habitual ritual practices.

33

Hans Castorp got "worse" during his visit to his cousin at The Elixir. No fair-minded person would deny this. Why did Hans get worse? In what sense did he get worse? These questions are difficult to answer. Perhaps it was simply that Hans could not tolerate feeling excluded. Put him with pot bangers and he'll bang pots. Put him with alcoholics and he'll do his best to drain the portable Fountain, no matter how much it hurts. This is the so-called "drunken chameleon" interpretation. Yes, Hans probably did feel a strong need to conform. For example, in the evening, after Group at the Quonset hut, after Flask Meditation, and shortly before the unstructured late-evening activities of unrehearsed and often never-before-heard-of conduct (referred to by residents as Mutant Sloughing), Mayor Jesse and Reverend Boyle would make the rounds of the residents living in the enormous, metal grain-elevator-turned-dormitory. It was a strange building. Hans, sitting alone in the Mr. Donut, would hear the grain elevator begin to hum. By 10:00 P.M. the building was essentially an enormous vibrating tuning fork set to a very high and painful pitch. It seemed to pick up inter-galactic radio frequencies and translate them up and down its length. The Mayor and the Reverend would talk to the residents and Hans could hear their noisy cajoling. They'd inquire into the effectiveness of the evening's activities; they'd lend a sympathetic ear and offer encouragement if the resident questioned his/her ability to walk; they'd offer to send Teddy or Timmy to fill the flask at the Fount if need be; and they'd generally admonish the resident on the importance of a sincere and complete involvement in The Elixir's unique energy dynamic ("Getting all the Way to Letting Go" or "Giving Up," as it was also known).

Although at one level such heart-to-hearts with either of these two men was the last thing Hans wanted, at another level he felt hurt and alone because his visitor status meant that the Mayor and Reverend left him out of their nightly rounds. And so, Hans began to undermine his visitor status by, as I have already mentioned, participating in an unvisitor-like way in rites such as Flask Meditation. The problem here was that he was simply not the sort of person who could spend a long career at The Elixir. To put it bluntly, he was a poor drunk. Alcohol did not taste like "the end of my problems" or "my best friend who would never let me down." No. Alcohol tasted to Hans like physical pain (headache and nausea), then like emotional pain (despair and confusion). Hans was one of those who, under almost any other conditions except the ones he found himself in, would never willingly touch a drop of liquor.

In spite of the difficulty with which he "drank his share," or perhaps I should say in spite of the physical pain through which he drank his share, he was beginning to fit in. He was becoming a "mate." At home. Comfortable and broken in like a cot at the Salvation Army Shelter.

Perhaps the following conversation between Hans and Cecile will help explain the situation. They were seated together in Daffy's drinking coffee in the empty afternoon. She wanted to know how he was feeling. She was concerned, and for good reason.

Hans thought about it. "Well, on the one hand I'd say I'm feeling a lot better. But I'm not sure that that should make a lot of sense because there was nothing wrong with me when I arrived here. I just came to visit my cousin. Remember? Nonetheless, it seems that at every turn I experience something horrible and threatening to me. Even people like my cousin Ricky and the brilliant Professor Feeling . . ."

"You think he's brilliant?"

"Well, sure. Don't you?"

"Go on."

"Well, they say and do things that leave me feeling pretty shaky. This place may be salutary for the sick person, but for the well person, it is contagious." Hans beetled his brow. "But, perhaps what's being revealed is that I'm not well at all! That's the scary thing. I've been ill all these years and I didn't know it. Perhaps my experience here is simply making clear to me that I really needed the therapy. Like the Mayor says, 'Never saw a boy who couldn't use a little treatment.'" Hans put his head in his hands with a moan. "I'm so confused. I'm miserable, and yet I'm starting to like it here. I'm getting to the point where it's difficult to imagine my life without this place." He looked into Cecile's face. Her features were soft, sad, and caring. "May I confide in you?"

"Of course, dear boy."

Hans hesitated before he began. "Dear boy." There was something so nice about those words. They were therefore shocking to Hans. "You know, I'm beginning to think it's possible that I may not be able to stay here much longer. I may have to abandon my cousin. I may have to leave."

Cecile looked gently into Hans's eyes and laughed. "Hans, you couldn't abandon Ricky if you tried. Abandonment is not mathematical and it can't be squared. Someone who is already marooned can't be abandoned. Could you abandon a wandering asteroid in some distant galaxy?" Then she did something she'd never done before; she reached towards Hans and took his hand. "But if you want to leave, Hans," she said, "I will go with you."

"What?" replied Hans. "What?" He felt as if Cecile had taken a paving brick from her purse, asked him to close his eyes, and then reached across and smashed him in the face.

Hans's suffering was obvious. "Good lord," he said, "so much is happening and it is still only the first week."

Now it was Cecile's turn to be amazed. "First week, love? You've been here for over two months. Don't you remember the fax from the director of personnel at Caterpillar? Don't you remember that he said it was fine with him if you took an extra two weeks before beginning because your position had been eliminated? And that was six weeks ago. How can you believe that this is still your first week?"

Hans looked like some small, soft, furry animal beneath a great demolition boot. "I can believe this is the first week because I just got here," he whispered. Hans's ability to maintain the brave front leaked away. His face fell.

The next thing he knew, he felt something wholly unfamiliar circling his shoulders. It was arms. Hugging human arms. Cecile was hugging him. She rested her chin gently on top of his head. She patted his shoulder. She was making little cooing "there-there" sounds. "Dear Hans," she whispered in his ear.

Suddenly, outrage surged through Hans. The touching of hands had been bad enough. But now this. He felt powerful, in control, knowledgeable. He stood and shook off her embrace, bumping her chin with the top of his head. He was like Samson shirking iron chains. He stared at her, appalled.

"What are you doing? What can you possibly imagine you are doing? What is going on in your head? What gives you the right? How could you imagine that this is appropriate behavior? Don't touch me. Don't ever touch me again. Stay away from me. This is why tables have two sides. I sit on one side and you sit on the other. Do you see anyone else behaving like this? Does Ricky do this? No. He does not. He allows others their own personal space. I'm astonished. My God. You touched me!"

If Hans expected anything, he expected that Cecile, who had come to seem to him a monster of self-knowledge and self-possession, would know what to do with his tirade. She would treat it as a monolith treats a breeze. But her response was as surprising as her unwanted hug had been shocking. She collapsed, emotionally collapsed, right in front of him. She sat back down at the table and buried her head in her hands. Hans noticed that this collapsing pushed her breasts up making her cleavage even more conspicuous than it was ordinarily. He felt a vague stirring. He'd never seen anything like this before. What was it? He had the general notion, though, that he could have her breasts now. He could just take them in his hands. This was it, the manly opportunity itself. But Hans wasn't quite ready to act. He was too amazed. This mysterious woman with the motherly bosom and capacious brain had had a full emotional reaction to something Hans had said. No one had ever responded emotionally to him before. But here it was. He seemed to have hurt her. Imagine. Him. Little Hans. Hurting somebody. He was impressed with himself. He hadn't known that it was possible for him to say something that could make another person cry. And he really was quite certain that, if he wanted by God, the breasts could now follow spilling out into his cupped hands.

But he did nothing of the sort. To his credit, I suppose, he asked, "Cecile, what's the matter?"

"The matter is," [sob, sob] "that you have hurt my feelings, you idiot! I tried to be nice to you, I tried to express my feelings for you, and you turned on me!"

"I did?"

"Yes, of course you certainly did! Are you stupid?" she asked, sounding to Hans a little like Teddy. This was more like it.

"And so that's how you'd describe what I did to you?" he continued, "I turned on you and hurt your feelings?"

Cecile looked up in such amazement that it overran her sadness for a moment. Some of the little waves of auburn hair were damp and stringy at her temple. Hans couldn't help feeling contempt for her. "Are you teasing me? Are you making fun of me, you little monster?" she asked.

Hans pulled himself up stiff. "No, I'm not teasing you. I guess if you get right down to it, I'm trying to suggest something to you."

"What?"

"I guess I'm trying to suggest that you deport yourself more like everyone else here. You don't see a lot of hugging going on. A lot of touching. I think there are laws on the books. You sure don't see Ricky hugging people. Why don't you act more like Ricky?"

Cecile visibly pulled herself together. It was such a violent physical effort that you could almost imagine that you saw the ropes and pulleys as she straightened in her chair.

"Well, Hans, since your cousin Ricky is a young man to whom it has not yet occurred that the cosmos does not circle round his erect penis like adoring children with brightly colored ribbons going round a Maypole, your suggestion that I be more like him will not be a simple suggestion for me to follow. No, it would be quite difficult and perhaps unpleasant. How could I, a modestly older woman, imagine what it's like to be a man in a nearly constant state of sexual arousal?"

Hans was outraged at this comment. "What on earth do you mean?"

"What I mean is that if you have the use of the eyes in your head you can see that there is always with your cousin a vertical rupture straight up his denims. Are you trying to tell me that you've never noticed? It's never seemed odd to you? That malicious grin off the silver teeth of his zipper?"

This is how Cecile spoke when she was angry, and Hans had made her angry.

"No. I've never noticed this."

"Well, try looking and you'll see that your dear cousin's penis is almost constantly erect, that it pushes out the material of his jeans, and that when the light catches his zipper in the right way it looks like teeth."

"But this is impossible. How can he stay aroused all of the time?"

Cecile was becoming increasingly impatient with this boy, our Hans. "There are devices for such things, you know. I would think that even a lost soul such as you are might have heard of them. Straps? Soft gadgets? Velcro attachments? No?" Hans shook his head in a sad "sorry." Cecile continued, "In any event, Ricky is not in need of them. He maintains his priapic achievement without the aid of artificial stimulants. It's sheer force of rigid will. But I wouldn't call it arousal. No, not that. A human being could almost understand that. It's more on the order of a statement. Who he is. What he's capable of. This fact is the very spine of his legendary status around here."

"How do you know all this?"

Cecile blushed. "Well, everyone knows it."

"Everyone? I didn't know it."

Now Cecile just laughed. She laughed and laughed. Something was very funny. Unable to control her laughter, Cecile got to her feet. Then a new course of sobs launched from her. She staggered away leaving Hans sitting alone.

"And just what the hell is a Blue Peter?" he called after her.

But Hans was not quite alone. The ubiquitous Professor Feeling had been sitting quietly at a table off to their side the whole time. He'd witnessed the whole depressing conversation. But for Hans, it was as if he'd just appeared like some blood-sucking apparition.

Feeling said, "You know, lad, without ever saying so, a woman like that could quite cordially hate you for what you have just done."

Hans groaned. She was his only friend. He thought of Cecile's wavy auburn hair of the long-ago style, the prominent rounded cheekbones, the narrow eyes. He thought of her smile. Her general May Queen beauty washed over him. Hans hated the thought that he'd just ruined his relationship with her. Now that face would never be his.

"Indulging in romantic regrets about the lovely Frau X will do little good, young friend. You fucked up." Feeling tapped the ash of his cigarette onto the floor.

Just then little Teddy came walking up to Hans's table wiping his chubby hands on his T-shirt. So much old food and gore clung to the T-shirt that it looked like it had been dipped in an abattoir vat and put on Teddy to dry.

"Don't tell me," said the little man, looking things over, "he fucked up again."

Feeling smiled softly. "What we used to call a 'contretemps,' Teddy."

"Oh I saw 'em out here and I knew something was going on. What was it this time? More of his liberal baloney? Another day in the cloud-cuckoo-land of how he thinks things ought to be?"

"You might say."

Little Teddy came right up under Hans's shoulder. He smelled like a french-fry vat. "Did she offer to take you back to the Mr. Donut?" The most awful, evil leer came to his ketchup-spattered face. "Did she offer to take your little pee-pee in her hands right here under the table?" Teddy put his obscene, lard-soaked hand on Hans's thigh. Teddy seemed like a creature made all of beef tallow.

Hans jumped up from the table, near tears, while the Professor and Teddy broke up laughing.

"You're disgusting! You disgust me! All of you! It's repulsive! And evil! Your bodies! The unbelievable filth you speak!"

The Professor and Teddy looked at each other and nodded wisely. They'd never heard so much, so concisely put, coming from Hans. This was some sort of breakthrough.

"What do you people want from me? What are you trying to do to me?" Hans cried. "I feel like you have some awful sort of plans for me, but I don't know what they are."

"Hans," said Feeling, "it's okay. Calm down. You're among friends. Your dearest friends. We just want you to relax now. That's all we ask. Nothing more. Just calm down." The Professor raised his chest and his pointy little beard and his beady little eyes in a big wide breath and exhaled. "There. See? Better. Relaxed. All relaxed. Deep breathing helps. You're so tense, you poor thing. You can't even understand when a little boy jokes with you."

"Yeah, I was just joking around, you big dummy."

"Teddy, please."

"Well," replied Hans, "it's just that I don't know, I never know, how to take you people. I can't tell the difference anymore. What's a joke? What's not? I don't know."

"That's cuz you're a liberal moron."

"Teddy, Mr. Castorp is not feeling well. Take it a little easy on him. He can't tell that you're really expressing affection for him."

"What! Are you kidding? I don't feel no affection for him!"

"For my part, I believe that it is as simple as this: Mr. Hans is feeling a vibrational imbalance." Feeling scrutinized Hans. "It is my personal belief that he has bad objects in his guts. Yes, no question. There is an intrusive, disgusting, dirty creature in him. That's why he says the things he does. Hans, listen to me. The disgusting things you see in us are really in you. Do you understand?" Feeling cocked his head and held out his hands in a solicitous way. "Could anything be a clearer corroboration of this thesis than your present state?"

"I doubt it, Doc," said Teddy.

"I believe he needs to be restored to life as a matrix of hope through a regressive union."

Teddy seemed to get very excited at this. His mouth opened wide, hardly daring to believe what he was hearing. "Regressive union! Are you kidding?"

"I don't kid about such things, Teddy."

"Right here?"

"The proper place to strive to accomplish a return to the garden of dual-unity is wherever you are at the moment."

Teddy threw his hands in the air. "Yay-hoo! The sucking doctor!" Then he sing-sang, bouncing with his hands in the air. "The sucking doctor, the sucking doctor, we're going to see the sucking doctor."

"What is this?" asked Hans, deeply suspicious.

"Medicinal sucking is like a magnet, Hans, that pulls out the patient's dirt. In this case, your disgust."

"You're kidding."

"No, he's not kidding you stupid fucking stupid head. He's the sucking doctor."

Suddenly, Teddy was tearing at Hans's shirt, trying to lift it.

"Stop it! Don't touch me! You're filthy! You're covered with ketchup and old french fries and I can't tell what else! I can't stand it!"

The Professor, calmly, "Ordinarily we would exchange clothing first, Hans, but because I can feel your intense need for an immediate sucking union, we will neglect that this time."

"No, oh no, you do not feel my need for anything! You're crazy!" He swatted at Teddy's hands, but the urchin was clever, quick and experienced.

"You have been feeling a loosening in your abdominal area. It is not unlike an ovarian discomfort."

"What are you talking about?"

Teddy had Hans's shirt stretched up above his chest. Hans's legs were pinned beneath the table by one of the benches. He was nearly bent over backwards. The Professor approached. He brushed his hands over Hans's stomach.

"'Pider webs!" he mewled.

"That's how he says 'spider webs' when he's the sucking doctor, Mr. Phony-Liberal-Full-of-His-Own-Stupid-Claptrap," explained Teddy.

"'Pider Webs! I brush them away with my fingers. I feel the bad objects in your guts. There are pebbles just beneath your skin." Feeling looked Hans sternly in the eye. "Now, I am going to return you to life."

And he ducked his head towards Hans's belly. Teddy released a banshee scream. The Professor's lips were dark and shaped like a maelstrom.

"A-bbbbbuuuuuuuhhhhhhhhhh."

In her distant dormitory, Cecile paused in her weeping when she heard a scream crawl to her side. She sat right straight up when it was followed by a deafening giggle.

34

Having now internalized all of Hans's most private pain through his "regressive union," having sucked them up, Professor Feeling was now in a position to tell the children the story of how Hans came to be Hans.

"And from that day forward, children, I knew all of little Hans's deepest secrets. For I had taken them inside myself.

"For example, I know about the day of Hermann Castorp's sixty-fifth birthday. Mr. Castorp was the father of seven children, one of whom was twelve-year-old Hans. He and his wife lived in a dingy townhouse in a world of dingy townhouses. The only discernible success of this building was that it was a cubicle. That is, it successfully resisted two dimensionality. Quite an accomplishment in that squalid, evil little place. Not every home succeeded. Many people really lived in a façade. It was like living in a sheet of cardboard. The Castorps had lived there for the last ten years, since Hermann Castorp's final attempt at gainful employment.

"But Hermann's sixty-fifth birthday was a special, special occasion. Family and friends packed the tiny home. The highlight of the evening was the almost constant consumption of alcohol by the men. It started with vodka and orange juice, wine with dinner, and then whatever remained of the vodka after dinner and forget the damned orange juice.

"Two large bottles of vodka had been brought as presents honoring the unlikely (in this case) if not unprecedented occasion of a man's sixty-fifth birthday. Curtis, Hans's brother-in-law, nestled a half-gallon of Golden Gate vodka into Hermann's arms like a sleeping baby. Aaahh! Mrs. Castorp commented that these were nice presents. She placed the other bottle heavily on a table to which the men gravitated immediately, grunting in that pure way that men grunt when they sense an impending drunk-fest. Curtis was the first one there, pouring himself a salubrious water glass full to the brim.

"By eleven o'clock, Hermann was unable to get up out of his chair. Every few minutes, a friend or family member would bend over, peer into his deep blue eyes and say, 'How you doin', Hermann? How you doin'? Are you enjoyin' your birthday party?' Then they'd refill his glass and comment on what a nice time everybody was having.

"Shortly before midnight, just before people began to leave, Hermann's youngest boy, twelve-year-old Hans, walked into the living room clad in his cowboy pajamas, frowning deeply. He went directly to his father's side, picked up the bottle of vodka and walked back toward his room with it. Hermann watched Hans do this and seemed at first startled and confused. He tried to get up and give chase, but that option had been eclipsed around nine-forty-five. So in a voice soaked in rage and hurt, he bellowed, 'He took my birthday present! Hans took it! Bring it back to me, Hansy!'

"He looked around the room seeking the concerned eye that might mean help. Hilda castorp, worried, walked briskly away looking for

Hans and the misappropriated bottle. Curtis went over to his father-in-law and said, 'It's okay, Dad. Don't worry. Mom will get your birthday present back.'

"Soon Hilda returned with the vodka saying, 'It's okay now, Hermann. Hans doesn't understand. He's too young to understand.'"

35

Ricky and the Mayor were seated on blue plastic milk crates in the bare dirt in front of the Farmer's Bank of Pontiac. It was dawn. The sun's light seemed confused about whether its job was to reveal or hide things. Between them, sprawled in the dirt, was Teddy. He was asleep or passed out or dead. His pants were falling off and his T-shirt pulled up, revealing his back. A single, fat, bluebottle fly made daring forays to the saliva at Teddy's chin before dashing back to the safety of his shoulder. The Mayor and Ricky were silent. They looked down on Teddy as if he were the image of a martyred holy figure.

Then from the direction of the Quonset hut Professor Feeling came strolling up, hands in his pockets. He surveyed the scene. What have we here? He thought. He pulled a milk crate out from a stack of five and seated himself leaning back against the rough, infectious brick of the Farmer's Bank of Pontiac. After a moment, he nudged Teddy's little body with the toe of his leather boot.

"Somber, somber, heh-heh," Feeling chuckled quietly, lighting a meditative cigarette with a chrome lighter shaped and monogrammed just like The Elixir's flasks. "You know, gentlemen, this little scene reminds me of nothing so much in the world as the Law of Karmic

Return. 'What goes around comes around.' Splat in your face, gentlemen. Splat in your face."

Feeling pulled his fingers through his damaged and graying shoulder-length hair. Ricky and the Mayor continued their quiet and dispassionate sitting, as if they had decided this was the posture in which they would end their lives.

"You know, I too used to be part of the Daily Illusion. I was on payroll or parole, something, I'm not quite clear about it now. I had a wife, oh God, did I have a wife. The Old Black Tongue, as she was known. Yes, where another man's wife might say, 'Good morning, love, how are you?' she'd say, 'Oh, it's you again. Back so soon?' Or, 'Once a fraud always a fraud.' Such morning rituals raised some grave self-esteem issues for me, gentlemen.

"This notion created by the Black-Tongued-One, She-of-the-Ebony-Glottis, that I was some sub-species of 'fraud,' came about because of her discovery of my auto-tantric meditation device. In the morning I would retreat to my study to work. Work it out. What my work produced was Insight, which does its silent and secret work in concealment. I created serenity, the controversy over which will soon circle the globe. I discovered Equipoise, which thinks God's thoughts for Him. I discovered Bliss, which allowed me to know that even if I were a fraud I was at least true. And I discovered Being, which informed me in clear terms that the accumulated mass of all the world's humans together exceeds the combined mass of all the world's other animals put together. Being wept while telling me this.

"I discovered that if I sat in lotus position with a tumbler of vodka or some other spirit by my side (a particular of sweeping import) my engagement in, my willingness to persevere, perfervid, in long mornings of meditation was greatly increased. Dramatically increased. I felt I was becoming the pure genie, a spirited intelligence that suffuses the littered cosmos, and that I had been this spirited intelligence all along, potentially. Of course, She-of-the-Black-Tongue could not see it this way, she could in fact barely see at all through the haze of her trite thoughts. Her repeated discoveries of me at meditation—the room ethereal with the evaporations of neutral grain spirits—prompted within her sincerely expressed, severely felt degrees of contempt, which contempt she often gladly shared with me thusly:

"'You are not a mystic. You are a drunk. See? This is vodka. This is a glass of vodka. You are a sponge of vodka. You are a rummy. Get it?'

"Etcetera. Well, my friends, I am from Kankakee, Illinois. I was, I assure you, the very first person from that metropolis ever to consider the notion of transcendence. So, for my own wife to undermine my most strenuous and inventive spiritual efforts . . . I had to ask myself, what does the Black-Tongued-One deserve? Or, so that my actions might not look like mere revenge, what does a black-tongued one create, opposite herself, as her own fate, solely because she has a black tongue? It was a Karmic question, and it was my deepest obligation and pleasure to find an answer."

Professor Feeling paused to look at his peculiar audience. Ricky sat most opposite him, his hard body making his milk crate creak and bend beneath him. He seemed a little dazed, and Professor Feeling was not optimistic that he was paying much attention to his story, or that he even recognized it as a story. He may not have recognized Feeling's account as human speech at all. Mayor Jesse, on the other hand, gestured and moved his lips constantly. Perhaps His Honor thought that he was telling this story. His dull pantomime was punctuated by grunting little piggy laughs, and wheedling gestures with a hand whose stubby fingers seemed nearly to drip with some black and unctuous deposit beneath the nails. Teddy had not as yet stirred. Feeling's deepest wonder was reserved for the inert Teddy. Feeling rocked a little more quickly on his crate and resumed.

"Well, it was at about this time that the karmic truth was revealed to me through the bodies and gestures of the women around me. These women were friends, wives of friends, colleagues, students, and simple women who stood waiting for me with their well-caparisoned rumps, their thighs like buttery capons, at the numerologically revealed street corners of our town. I discovered these street corners by hanging a bottle of Gilbeys out the window of my automobile as I drove by. Once I looked back at my car's rear seat to discover that there were no fewer than five of them there, their bodies running one into the other, patient, obliging and juicy.

"The cosmos's karmic obligations to my wife, completing the logic of her own actions (and not my 'clownish lusts,' the actions of an 'alcoholic sex fiend' as the legal depositions of the plaintiff's camp claimed) was to introduce these aforementioned more appreciative others to the curious delights of my tantric rites. And I did this thing . . ." Feeling's rocking on his milk crate became more promiscuous. ". . . Yes, I did these things again and again. I was successful to the following exceptional degrees.

"The wife of a colleague in astrophysics gave me moist oral gratuities in the front seat of a Ford Fiesta while our respective mates dozed off a Thanksgiving meal. A brilliant Jewish scholar of Nietzschean woes revealed to me the stupendous dangling lobes of her labia, which hung like velvet ears down the inside of her thighs. A Bengal poetess of unlimited self-deception (whose self-deception made deceit superfluous) downloaded the wisdom of the Upanishads directly from the uranium-rich fuel rod that I solemnly offered in her family's den while her husband ground herbs for garam masala in the kitchen. And then, rounding out this season of karmic balance, there was the teenager, daughter to the New York Stock Exchange, who introduced me to student-sized quantities of beer, peeing one's pants with cool aplomb, more orgasms than days, wrists bound to bed frames, and the bottomless consolation of her breasts which dangle to this day before my eyes.

"What I hadn't quite understood, what karmic law had still to teach me, was that what goes around comes around, sure enough, any drunk can provide this instruction, but this law also taught that what goes around comes around and then goes around again. Witness the morning on which I burst upon the teenage heiress's night before, with the thespian boy, the pretty Shakespearean, who had swallowed all of my future succor with his greedy lips. He was great, lengthy, naked, white and smooth like an unearthed grub. Yes, he was the great white worm of legend. And she, the dark heir to the American stock market's future, huddled in his arms like some furry creature seeking warmth in the most unlikely places.

"I calmly walked over and reached down and removed the eyeball of the shiny Shakespearean, which turned out to be no eyeball at all but the lynch-pin to the cosmos' order. Imagine a long train, hundreds of cars, where the coupling between each car is simultaneously undone, and each car has now its own violent fate. No sense. Relation. Any other car. Plucked up and dispersed. We were.

"The musty-smelling student apartment, the beer-soaked orange shag carpet more pizza than fabric, the urine and sperm soggy mattress over which one had formerly laughed, the scent now smelling of one's own grave, all this was caught up and sent whirling like some elemental force of nature, like satellites with nothing to orbit about. The Jewish theorist, and the poetess of charming side-long glances, and somebody else's wife whose lips sucked with a haunting disregard, all now whirled about as if we'd been at the zero ground of an engineering disaster which sent us hurtling out into zero gravity. Young girls hung to street signs as if they were caught in a tornado, or were tetherballs, crying, begging for me to stop, asking for more Gilbeys. All this spun slowly before me. And I confessed to Mother Maya: I MADE THIS. I *MADE* THIS. I MADE THIS FUCKING THING. IT IS ALL MY DOING, AND IT IS MY DOOR TO WHICH THIS DOG HAS COME TO DIE."

Abruptly, Feeling was done. He looked at his stunned congregation. No hosannahs today. He began to get up, as if to leave. Then he paused, poised on the edge of his milk crate. He seemed puzzled. He looked down at little Teddy. "Inquiring minds want to know," said Feeling. He laughed. Then he looked quite serious again. He reached forward with the toe of his boot and nudged Teddy's body. The boot made a little white dent in Teddy's hip. But Teddy did not rouse. Across the street, the corn plants lined up like good soldiers but so tightly that they might have been in a cattle car headed for the crematorium. The leaves of the stalks whispered drily in the wind. Shhhh . . .

With an awful grimace, Feeling pulled back his boot and kicked chubby Teddy in the thigh, shoving his legs over, and leaving an arc of raked dirt behind. Maybe there was a moan this time, like that from a stupified cherubim after a month's saturnalia. Feeling shrugged. What difference did it make? He stood and walked away, leaving behind Ricky, the Mayor, the little messiah and their obscene crèche. No sooner was he out of earshot than Mayor Jesse shuddered like a doll that we suspect comes to life the moment we leave the room. Now his fingers pointed left and right, he wiped a gout of spit from his chin, he called to unseen persons, he chortled, he mugged, his face condensed to a dot then banged out big as a bean field. He blinked like something that merely aspires to consciousness. And he said, "Professor, dang, you do have a way! Am I right on this? Hal? Whaddya think? But, jeez, Hal, that sunrise. Lord, it's hard on a man. Purty? You think that's purty, Hal? What's purty about it? Dang! Hal, hit that dimmer switch, would you man, this sun thing is gettin' to me."

36

The previous day. Whatever that means. The night of the day before. Sunset not sunrise. Whatever that means. Hans found himself stuck in the middle of it. Like a totem pole. The sun was ever the excitable boy dropping in the west. Hans perspired in his native polyester. After the days or weeks or months or whatever it was that he'd been there, the synthetic material of his shirt—had he remembered to change it even once?—was starting to dissolve in an awful stink. His feet sunk in sun-softened asphalt on the street opposite the Mr. Donut. The odd assortment of edifices stretched end-to-end, as weird to him as on his first day. He understood, his understanding merely abstract, that some forms of human intelligence might be grateful—or might simply enjoy—the warmth of the sun. And gentle air. For the air was gentle. Excuse him, but these notions were not coming to him without conscious effort. He had to concentrate in order to recognize the warmth of the sun.

Hans stood transfixed on the far side of the road, in front of his Mr. Donut, as a flow of men walked quickly by him full of a sad and strange necessity, faces forward, no one speaking, heading toward the distant Quonset hut into which they ducked with silent nods. It was the first time Hans had seen the mass of The Elixir's residents. They were almost all men. Some of them were young, their arms festering with tattoos. There was a wandering, desperate, edgy look in their rattled eyes. Others wore fraternity caps on backwards and T-shirts with mottoes like, "Fear is for pussies." They seemed angry and, oddly, arrogant. It was an arrogance without reason. An arrogance that came from one defeat after another. There were older men, slower, uncomfortable in human skin. They were beaten where the younger were eager. They had realized that of which youth was merely an anticipation. For them, the beast in the jungle had arrived, slowly, over time, but now—obviously—it was sitting bare-ass-down on their faces. These older men had their hands in their pockets. They sauntered sadly. They mumbled into the air, "Now listen to me . . . listen to me," like a mantra.

Once in a while, a pocket of children with one crazed woman in their middle would scurry by. Their faces were the elongated faces of well-beaten animals. The women were frightened. Their fear ran in every direction. They were afraid that a child would get lost. They were afraid that a man would seize one of the children. They were afraid that one of the children would notice something about the men. They were afraid one of the children might speak. The children too were headed for the doors of the Quonset hut into which dark they ducked submissively, their mothers pushing insistently at their shoulders.

Then out of the crowd Ricky came up to Hans. "Coming, Cousin?" He took him by the arm. "It's time." Hans's heart gave a sudden, melodramatic beat, without rhythm, of its own accord, as if it knew something it had no other way of communicating to its owner. Hans stared at his cousin. It was as if he dared to look at him for the first time. There was something hopeless about it. It was as if he were a citizen of the Empire and he merely wanted to know what the conquering Visigoth really looked like in the moment before the barbarian eviscerated and ate his organs. One supposes that there is a sort of odd courage in this. His gaze went slowly, despairing, his eyes drifting down the front of Ricky's trousers. Yes, there it was, just as Cecile had said. The steel teeth of Ricky's zipper ripped outward like something that would eat you. A gruesome smile.

"How many months, Cousin," asked Hans, "how many months have I been here and not dared to look at the mouth that would eat me?"

"What? What are you talking about?" Ricky tightened his grip on Hans's arm and jostled him. "What's up? Let's go. It's time. It's high time and then some."

"I'm not going," said Hans. "I'm going to take a walk."

"You're what?"

"I'm not going."

"Oh, you're going. You're going all right. It's time."

"I intend to take a walk."

"Shit. A walk. What kind of talk is that? Well, that really burns me, Cousin." Hans thought that now he would be punished. This sort of unruly behavior wouldn't be tolerated. Unpredictably, Ricky seemed to abandon his idea and laughed, as if he had been given a private audience to a future that was all comic futility.

"Well, old boy, don't overdo it. That's my advice. It's not the same here, you know."

Ricky's mastery of this place, his total comfort within it, infuriated Hans. He had the tormenting notion that Ricky could see the end of whatever path he, Hans, took. And all paths seemed to lead, he greatly feared, to this same place, to this soft depression in the asphalt where he presently stood.

Hans flared with desperate resistance. "Now listen to me. You can see that I can't go on like this. I've had enough. Really. Right up to here. I believe that my very blood is going to sleep. It's different with you. You belong here. You've accepted this. But me, I feel like my character is a lock that someone has changed the combination to. Without telling me. Get it? Don't worry, I won't try to take you away from your cure. I really won't. My aunt will just have to be disappointed. But it occurs to me that healthy people ought to go for a walk in the evening if the weather allows. I think they say it's salubrious. But we should not huddle together in a Quonset hut. There's nothing healthy in that. I can't say why I think this, but I do."

Ricky saw that nothing short of beating his cousin could change his mind. Beating his cousin would have been easy enough to do, but Ricky also understood that it would have been redundant.

Instead, he rejoined the crowd heading toward the hut, shouting back at his cousin, "Don't overdo it. That's my advice."

Hans had no idea what his cousin meant by "overdoing it." How do you overdo a walk? At the same time, he was beginning to feel something ominous about this stroll he proposed. Maybe it wasn't an escape but only a deferral of the inevitable. Hans made his first difficult steps into the stream of men. They trudged like miners on the way to the morning shift at the black, anthracite coal shaft. (In fact, many of them had a sooty caste to their faces, although that was probably just from cigarettes and filthy pillows.) Eventually, after crossing the current of men, he arrived at the path that led between the Mr. Donut and the Farmer's Bank, past stunted mulberry bushes, and over the narrow creek whose source seemed to flow up from beneath Daffy's. In a moment Hans was between the first two slag heaps which locals called The Desiccated Sisters. But, strangely, standing there as if he were a ticket vendor to some odd sideshow, or maybe it was Tomorrowland, was little Timmy, the intense urchin to the myriad Aunts Pearl of Caring Caravan, Inc.

"Hey, where you going?"

Hans grimaced.

"I'm going for a walk." Taking a walk was beginning to feel like the bravest thing he had ever done.

"Not so fast, slim. No one goes for walks around here."

"Well, I'm going for a walk."

"Well. La-dee-dah. Vertebrae among slimy creatures, eh? All right. Don't let me get in the way. I'm nothin' special in these parts. Go right on ahead." And he gestured for Hans to pass with a theatrical flourish.

Hans paused and turned on the little man. "And what do you have to say for yourself? Why aren't you going to the morning meeting?"

"Me? This morning I'm cultivating a knack for recognizing humorous moments."

Timmy smiled.

"Hey," he continued, "I think this is one!" He laughed. "Yep, this is one! Danged if it ain't!" Now he laughed with insult. "A God damn funny moment."

Hans pushed past him, splashing through the creek, agitating the potato peels that floated in it.

"Hey, Mr. Hans. One more thing," Timmy shouted through his laughter, "Fuck you and your kind. Ha ha ha ha ha ha ha ha ha ha!"

Hans gulped in the heavy, humid air and entered again the concavity between the cindery slopes of The Desiccated Sisters. Hans's chest expanded with an accelerating rush that he mistook for excitement. He had this dim hope that by pressing beyond the dry boundaries of The Elixir, he might enter an alternate world. Maybe he even imagined that Nature waited to embrace him. But we know that this was naive. We may shake our heads sadly. Truly is it said, a person is not diseased because the world in which he finds himself is whole and healthy. The corollary of the "Family as Drunk" is "The World as Weed." The bare flanks of The Desiccated Sisters, whose rocky tits thrust up stupidly, and the forest of naturally bonsaied maples and oaks led not to a verdant bower, an attractive and utopian alternative to the suffocating reign of The Elixir, but to Central Illinois. Hans had entered a Nature-free Zone, so established by the mighty Council of a Thousand Drinks. Zero tolerance. He entered the Land-as-Factory. Every square inch burdened with intent. Everything bleared and smeared with ill-conceived toil. He stepped into it and oil oozed around his step. Here the parks were all potted plants. Nothing lived here but the pigeon, starling, sparrow, spider, cockroach, mouse, moth, fly and weed, and the bosses lamented the existence of even these and made plans to exterminate them.

Then, lo, there at the end of his path, on a dry lip looking out over the stunted cornfields of the once-fertile long-stem prairie, was a figure clad all in black. He looked like a conductor leading his orchestra. But he was the Right Reverend Phenues Boyle in all his righteous glory.

He was blacker than the sooty air, dressed in his pitchy vestments like it was Sunday or some other dark occasion. And when Boyle raised his arms in the air, there returned the great stink. The stinking wind. Boiling tennis balls. Beach thongs in chicken fat. Simmering household appliances. He seemed to conduct these smells like a great orchestra. Boyle smiled and nearly frightened young Hans to death.

From the Reverend's perch, high up among the slag heaps, you could see thrown before you the whole of the previous century, the noxious and notorious twentieth.

"Friends," said Boyle, gesturing as if he were leading the brass section into the final movement of some sort of Wagnerian mess of a symphony, "Can't you feel it? That itching in your hearts? It's a dandelion taking root, rooting down!

"Dear friends, millions of royal penguins on Macquarie Island are being boiled and rendered into oil—a pint per bird. I stand here alone among the ferns and skunk cabbage in a bowl of old light. Summer-nesting ducks guard their nestlings back in the reeds. I take a crescent wrench and span each little head to see if it's fit for the world at the world's end."

Starlings descended from the obscure blue and perched on the Reverend's squared shoulders as if he were a scarecrow. "C'mon out here, Son," he said, wriggling the bones of his fingers at Hans. "I want you to see something. This'll all be yours some day. C'mon, now."

He gestured emptily but received no response, enthusiastic or otherwise, from Hans.

"I don't think you're payin' attention, boy. Lookit! The brick, the asphalt, the concrete, the dancing signs and garish posters, the feed and excrement of the automobile, the litter of its inhabitants: they compose, they decorate, they line our streets, and there is nowhere, nowadays, our streets can't reach."

But Hans didn't need literally to look in order to know "what would all be his some day." In the foreground, the corn factory. Six-hundred kernels per ear, twenty-thousand ears per acre, closer to infinite than any other thing Hans had ever seen. Then, rising to the horizon, the enormous hog confinement facilities, silhouetted against the pinkish sky. Fifty-thousand hogs lamenting as if each were the one into which Christ had thrown the demoniacs. The vast lagoons of waste, rivaling the Great Lakes, simmering, the effluvia at a low boil. Finally, beyond that the glow of the vast Chicago-Aurora-Joliet downtown nexus. Hans could feel the land sinking under it all.

But it could just have been his heart.

Hans turned to trudge back to the compound. The Reverend's voice chased him. "Now, boy, don't be like that. Don't feel that way. That's no way for a boy to be. We need you. We need you. You're a team player and this is a team. Look here what I got for you! What's this? Do you know? Mmmm, good! Do you know what's in this bag? I'll tell you. Pork rinds! Salted, too. See how these devilish birds eat 'em up?" He handed the snacks to the starlings on his shoulders. "What's that tell you? Why, they're good! And good for you. So c'mon back. I'll share 'em with you. Hey, it's lonely out here." The Reverend's feet had, as legend claimed, been nailed to the wooden platform on which he stood. "Say, hey, are you payin' attention? Can you hear? Am I speakin' English? Do you know what's good for you? Don't make me tell you twice. Well, then the heck with you, you ungrateful wretch. Won't spend a moment with his old dyin' daddy. Kinda boy are you, anyway? Good for nothin' is what kind!"

When Hans arrived back at The Elixir, everything was quiet. He could feel the Quonset hut pulsing in the distance. He felt isolated. He heard a muted psalm on the wind, "A mighty fortress is our Lord." Hans had no idea what this might apply to. He approached the Mr. Donut from the rear, coming up the dirt path.

When he entered the building, he noticed that the door that had always been locked, the door which read, "No Admittance Employees Only," was wide open, as if someone were trying to get some fresh air down there. The door led to the basement, from which all of the maddening sounds had come. The same basement which had the weird electrical tie-in with household appliances. His neighbors. He could now know who they were. If he dared.

He peeked around the corner. It looked dark. As his eyes adjusted, though, he could see that there was some sort of glow down there. The edges of the stairs caught just enough of the glow that Hans could descend. He went down, carefully. Slowly. At the bottom of the stairs, he turned a corner and saw that the basement was finished. There was carpeting and furniture. The faint blue-gray light was from an antique television set that was playing an old black-and-white show. The sound was soft, nearly inaudible. Carefully, he felt his way to the couch facing the TV and sat. It was James Arness as Matt Dillon in *Gunsmoke*. He was talking in a grim, articulate way to a pale, whiskered man. The man's face twitched with the effort to understand what Sheriff Dillon said. Hans settled back. The TV light played across his face and flashed in his eyes. Hans's mouth hung open. Hans liked this old show. It was comforting.

Then, to Hans's left, there was movement. Something rose half out of a recliner. It was an enormous apparition. It was staring at Hans, but Hans did not seem alarmed. Perhaps this ghost was here to ask Hans to do something for him. To exact some revenge. Hans was ready.

"Is that you, Hansey?"

"Yes, it's me, Dad."

"Been out late?"

"Yes, Dad. I was out with my friends."

"Have a good time?"

"Yes. It was fun."

"Didn't get into any trouble, did you?"

"No, Dad. We just went to a drive-in movie."

"What was it?"

"What was what?"

"The movie."

"*Cool Hand Luke.*"

"That one with Paul Newman?"

"Yeah, that's the one."

"Well, I'm glad."

"What have you been doing, Dad?"

"Just watchin' TV."

"*Gunsmoke*, huh?"

"Yep."

"You really like that show, don't you."

"Yep."

"You watch it every night."

"It's on every night on this channel. This special channel that they have for me with my shows on."

"Some of these you must have seen hundreds of times."

"Not hundreds."

"But lots."

"Lots, sure."

"Well, I think I'll leave you alone. Don't want to bug you."

"Why, you're not bothering me! Sit down and watch the cowboy show."

"Think I'll go to bed."

"Okay, then, buddy. Nighty-night. I'll see you in the morning."

"Okay, Dad."

Hans walked slowly back up the stairs and into his room. He went over to his bed. Teddy was there watching TV, a remote control device gripped between his two immature hands. He pointed and squeezed the buttons as if he were trying to force toothpaste out of it. The show he watched carried pornographic images that accelerated and froze then accelerated again with each push of the button. A jiggly woman with flouncing breasts. A man whose body was itself like an enormous muscular erection. The woman was getting fucked from behind. Hans assumed that the man was Ricky. "Of course," thought Hans. "And the woman is dear Cecile. Never doubted it, really." So this was it, the distinguished thing itself. All of his hopes and fantasies reduced to this, a little black spot. All the questions and uncertainties at last answered. That's all she was, a mean little black spot. All, really, that he could see of the woman was her buttocks, so there might have been some room for doubt. How could he be so sure, given this perspective? What did he know, after all, of Cecile's buttocks? And yet, sure he was. Well, at least he had been cleansed before he had to see this, the end of his illusions. Sucking doctor did it. Cleansed him. Made it all okay. Not dirty anymore. Or so dirty that he'd emerged on dirt's far side, implausibly clean. Hans turned his stare on Teddy. Eventually, Teddy looked back at Hans.

"What are you lookin' at, stupid?" asked Teddy.

No response. Hans didn't have to respond to anything anymore. He was done with that. Teddy's eyes glowed red in the dark as if he were a household pet caught by a flashbulb.

"That's Ricky and Cecile, isn't it?"

"What? Have you lost your mind? I found this video out by the Atrazine dump. This was made a million years ago. Look at them. Nobody fucks like that anymore. He's still got his socks on. Probably both dead by now, whoever they are. Oh, by the way, we're out of juice."

"You're a liar. You're all liars. I'm the last one to see it, your lies. That's why you're here. To show this to me. It's part of your plan."

Hans stared at the images, but now Teddy stared at him, considering.

"Oh, I get it. Brother." He sighed profoundly. "Just my luck, I guess. Fucking liberals are all alike. You all come around in the end." He looked at Hans directly and asked, "You're one of them now, is that it?" No response. "Took you long enough. Loser."

And he turned back to the TV, his expression hard.

Later that night, Hans felt something digging into his neck. He couldn't sleep. He put his hand under the pillow. It was the gun

Ricky had given him. The gun needed for terrifying all the cab drivers. He pulled it out from beneath the pillow and looked at it. The gun's blackness was impressive even in the dark. It seemed even more intense than the dark of night. Then he remembered that it was made of licorice. Licorice was the darkest thing known to man, wasn't it? He stifled a giggle. He would take a bite of the licorice gun. Pretty hard!

Teddy growled at him. "Quit movin' around. You're waking me up."

Then Hans put the licorice gun to his temple.

At least he was pretty sure it was *his* temple.

Epilogue

Thus it was that one Hans Castorp was taken up by the world into which he had been born, just as we are all taken up in one way or another. I don't know how to unsay what's been said, or undo what's been done, or unworld what is beyond question the world. But let me relate one last story that at least suggests that not all stories condemn us to what we already know. It's a story from *The Big Book of Despair*, the volume Hans found in his Donut dormitory. Some group had distributed copies of the book all over The Elixir as if it were Gideon's Bible. Maybe this organization thought of itself as a sort of Johnny Appleseed distributing the dull pippin of anguish. It happened that Hans read this story one afternoon several years into his life, as it were, at The Elixir. To his credit, it made him sit up for a moment and wonder.

There was this guy who owned a Caddy. It was a big green monster of a Caddy and it had once been a real prize of a car (it had in fact been the guy's pride and joy), but now it was getting old. It leaked fluids onto the driveway, and the rings were shot. Consequently, it used so much oil that he thought he would have to hook up a funnel system through the front seat so that he could empty quarts of 10-30 into the bugger as he drove. Also, the heater leaked onto the floor and in the cool spring months astonishing mushrooms grew in profusion out of the carpeting. The experience of seeing the car go from new and valuable to old and an embarrassment was of course at first a disappointment to the guy. But soon he saw, because he was one of those guys who gets to see, that the disintegration of the Caddy provided an interesting lesson for him about investing self-esteem in objects all of which are not only illusory in and of themselves, but prone to, nay, certain to decay. So he actually kept the beast *because* it was old and decrepit and because it spoke to him, in an unmistakably clear, green voice, about an important wisdom. It also could still limp to the grocery store once or twice a week, even if it had to fart blackly the whole way.

But, to get on with this story, one day somebody stole his car right out of his driveway! Seems that the "classics" value of the '54 Caddy was going through the roof. And even limping as it did and sprouting fungi from its carpet, it was valuable for its near pristine body. When the guy's neighbor found out what had happened, he ran over (taking, as he ran, many a tossed look back at his own car, a brand-spanking new Chevy Corvair, whose presence suddenly seemed to him much more a matter of speculation than it had before this theft). He said, "I'm so sorry to hear about your car. I can't believe that some young punk" (he was a great one for blaming things on young punks) "has stolen your good ol' Caddy."

The guy looked at his neighbor and said, "You know, I can't tell if this is a good thing or a bad. The car was a piece of junk. I didn't dare leave the neighborhood in it. And my homeowner's policy, for some crazy reason clear only to insurance guys, is going to give me money for it, the kind of money you would expect to get for something that actually ran. I'm kind of surprised that the thief was able to convince it to drive off the block. On the other hand, I'll miss the things the Caddy taught me about life."

The neighbor looked at him in confounded confusion. "Don't you fucking get it? Some jackass young punk of a kid stole your automobile right off of your own private property. There are principles involved."

Some weeks later, he got a call from the police saying that they'd found the Caddy at a nearby used car lot and he could get it back. Also, the owner of the lot wanted to talk to him. So the guy took a bus to the lot and went immediately to his Caddy. He stuck his head inside and smelled the sweet decay of upholstery and smiled. Yes, he thought, this is my car. It's speaking to me. "Born alone, die alone, in between a dream." That's my car all right. He was glad. But he had more to be glad about.

The owner of the lot felt bad about being taken in by the thief (he described this thief in dramatic retrospect as a "fucking young punk"). He may also have wanted to seem above suspicion for the benefit of the police, who were taking the opportunity to check out some of the other used cars on the lot. So he said he wanted to make it up to the guy. He wanted to give him a newer car. (Okay, at first he just wanted to offer the guy a "real good deal" on a new and expensive car, but the guy was in no way interested in any factory discounted stock overload sticker rebated special leasing arrangements.) So the dealer ended up practically giving him a used Plymouth Barracuda, sporty as all get out, still pretty fast, and a real plunge back into memories of the guy's sleeker youth. At first, he thought he shouldn't take it. It would be yet another possession to worry about even if it was cheap to the point of free. But these sweet memories and the idea that his neighbor would never shut up if he turned down such a good deal finally convinced him to go ahead with it.

Now the guy's neighbor was amazed at his good fortune. "I can't believe this," he said, "someone robs you and you not only get the thing you lost back, but you get a new thing worth double or more the thing you supposedly lost! You are such a lucky stiff!"

The guy's neighbor really was getting a whale of a lesson himself, if he knew how to recognize it. But all he could recognize was that the guy's Barracuda made his Chevy Corvair (newer though it might be) look lumpish. His Corvair had no sporty wire wheels, for example. And the neighbor guy still had two more years of payments to make on his lumpish vehicle. (In truth, he'd gotten essentially mugged money-wise by his dealer who had nothing more difficult to do to make that sale than wipe the neighbor guy's drool off his chin. In further truth, with still a year left to pay on it, his Corvair would implode after a fan belt broke, the car over-heated, the block warped, the cylinder walls corrugated, the piston rings wore, and the apocalyptic flatulence of the little Corvair made the black farting of the guy's Caddy look like an azure day.)

But the guy himself was strangely uneasy, even worried about his good fortune. He wondered if this flashy Barracuda wasn't just another time-mutability trap like the Caddy before it. He really didn't want to have to worry about scratches and dings and shouting at strangers who parked too close to him. And he sure didn't see the pleasure in spending his weekends out in the driveway with a bucket of soapy water and a can of polish always anxious about something. Was it rusty? Was it shiny? Was it shiny enough? Was that a streak on the right rear panel? Strange, I know, but this guy was really different. He thought different thoughts than you and I. He was the kind of guy who understood that each mile that popped up on the odometer was a little death. ("I'll never travel that mile again. This machine is one mile closer to rusting in a junk yard.") And this was not morbidity talking to him. The guy actually took some sort of weird comfort in these thoughts. He must have been one helluva guy in his previous life.

So, anyway, a few weeks later, the guy's son (who, unhappily, possessed little of the guy's wisdom—so much for theories that past-life-wisdom is transferred genetically) took the car out for a spin. An unauthorized spin with the unauthorized ignition key, the unauthorized buddy and the way unauthorized six-pack of Olde English 800 malt liquor. He had a license and all but he was really ill-prepared for pushing a speedy roadster fast on country black-tops—like notoriously windy Cypress Road, where drunk high-school boys immemorial went to die—which is exactly where he pointed himself and his buddy, as if they had a sort of destiny.

Well, inevitably the guy's son crashed the danged car into a tree. He'd been swilling some beer and failed to notice a curve ("there were a lot of curves," he complained, "and I only missed one") and went into a big old cedar (second growth, but fifty-year-old second growth and more than big enough to shiver this kid's timber). Happily, it was a sort of glancing blow that more diverted than crushed the vehicle. The son and buddy weren't completely killed although both had numerous broken bones and cuts to their faces which flowed freely and terrified mothers for one hundred miles in every direction.

The neighbor, who was by this time starting to wear a path in the lawn with his frequent need to console/congratulate, came over to tell the guy how sorry he was. (Although, you know how these things go in the human brain, he wasn't entirely sorry to see how smashed up the guy's Barracuda was.) But the guy said, "I don't know how to feel about it. My son is going to be okay. The car is trashed, and I can't repair it because I didn't have collision coverage on it, but I'm sort of glad that I don't have to worry any more about how it will affect my life. Plus, if I leave it crippled in the driveway for the next few years it will serve as a constant reminder to my son. He needed the opportunity to learn. So who knows if this is good or bad news."

The neighbor retreated, muttering, back across the lawn to his own home, walking by his own frighteningly shiny Corvair. (He actually, for the first time, looked at it with some suspicion.)

Two years later, when the guy's son was draft age, he received a letter from the draft board telling him that it was time to serve his country. In Vietnam. So the poor dumb kid went down with hundreds of other poor dumb kids. But the guy's poor dumb kid failed the physical because his knees had some resemblance to knees but also to mashed potatoes, all thanks to one Barracuda and one cedar tree.

Again, the guy had to look at the situation and say, "If my son hadn't driven the Barracuda into a tree, he would be on his way now to Vietnam. Instead, he can go to college, if he can get into one with a 1.95 GPA. This is a great thing."

Of course, once he said that, cosmic laws of irony were set to spinning. The boy went to college where he met hippies and draft card burners and went to concerts at the Fillmore West and took a few consciousness expanding drugs which, given the constricted consciousness he took them with, couldn't help but do just that—expand his brain. So he came home with this new, expanded brain and lectured his father on imperialism and the military industrial complex and the CIA and the hypocrisy of the guy's generation and on and fucking on. So, once again, the guy was totally unsure about the good/badness of what had happened. He even wondered if he wouldn't rather have had his son shipped off to Nam. Or killed by the cedar. Or never born! But the guy was really getting quite wise about this nothing-completely-good-or-bad stuff. So rather than taking his son by his ponytail and smashing the hell out of him, he decided to build a sunroom on the back of his home. Lovely California sunlight streamed into that room. There's really nothing in the world like California sunlight. He filled the room with house plants (among them, a very stout, swart bonsai cedar!) and one squat chair. The chair was pointed at a little shrine into which he had built the severed front end of the old Caddy. And whenever he'd think that something good or bad had happened to him, he'd go into his sunroom and sit and look at the grill of the Caddy. Sometimes the grill would look like it was the angry, growling mouth of some predatory animal. At other times it looked like a very toothy and vaudevillian grin. Sometimes it was both at the same time.

Because of this, the guy frequently found himself laughing. Which was fine and hurt no one except that the guy's neighbor could hear him laughing and see him sitting in his weird little sunroom cracking-up over something, and he didn't know what it was about, but he wondered if the guy might not be laughing about him. And it started to drive him crazy. He fantasized about shooting the guy with a high-powered rifle right through the window of his freaky room (which would have been the ultimate test for the guy's philosophy). And he damned near did. He was getting that bugged about it. But he didn't. Instead, he packed up his shiny Corvair in which slept a smoggy future, sold his house and bought a nice not-yet-dented vinyl place out in the new subdivisions in Walnut Creek there to reside with thousands of others who, when their Chevy Corvairs self-destructed and farted blackly, would curse the car, its maker and their personal fates as very bad things indeed.

When the guy heard that his neighbor was moving, he didn't know if it was a good or bad thing. After all . . .

LANNAN SELECTIONS

The Lannan Foundation, located in Santa Fe, New Mexico, is a family foundation whose funding focuses on special cultural projects and ideas which promote and protect cultural freedom, diversity, and creativity.

The literary aspect of Lannan's cultural program supports the creation and presentation of exceptional English-language literature and develops a wider audience for poetry, fiction, and nonfiction.

Since 1990, the Lannan Foundation has supported Dalkey Archive Press projects in a variety of ways, including monetary support for authors, audience development programs, and direct funding for the publication of the Press's books.

In the year 2000, the Lannan Selections Series was established to promote both organizations' commitment to the highest expressions of literary creativity. The Foundation supports the publication of this series of books each year, and works closely with the Press to ensure that these books will reach as many readers as possible and achieve a permanent place in literature. Authors whose works have been published as Lannan Selections include Ishmael Reed, Stanley Elkin, Ann Quin, Nicholas Mosley, William Eastlake, and David Antin, among others.